# PROGRAMMED

# PROGRAMMED

## Mike Monczunski

| | | |
|---|---|---|
| Library of Congress Control Number: | | 2024910765 |
| ISBN: | Softcover | 979-8-3694-2316-5 |
| | eBook | 979-8-3694-2317-2 |

**To order additional copies of this book, contact:**
Xlibris
844-714-8691
www.Xlibris.com
Orders@Xlibris.com
860555

# CONTENTS

# CHAPTER ONE

*D*IE *BROTCHENSTELLE* IS SERGEANT JÜRGEN Detweiler's daily first stop. Inhaling fresh coffee and warm baked goods, he nods curtly at the familiar faces waiting in line.

*"Please respond to a one ten about bodies at the Frauen Helfen Zentrum."*

The shrill alert quiets the café, a woman stops sipping tea, a suited businessman slowly lowers his newspaper.

Stern faced, Detweiler unhooks his belt radio.

"I'm on the way."

Customers step aside as he hurriedly leaves the line.

Their curious faces follow his Polizei cruiser zipping past the café's window with lights flashing.

"Is that an abortion clinic?" the businessman asks.

"Yes, it's by the Red-light district." the woman answers.

Anxious hushed conversations sweep through the café.

◆◆◆◆◆

His flashers left on, Detweiler flings his door open.

A brunette in a beige pantsuit and high heels waits for him with a horrified face.

"Oh my God, oh my God!" she screams through her hands.

Detweiler unsnaps his holster.

"Where are they?"

She doubles over with coughing spasms, her trembling hand waving to the clinic entrance.

"Where inside?" he barks.

"In his office."

He brushes past her, ignoring her choked vomiting.

---

Gripping his pistol, Detweiler gently pushes the door.

Skinny ribbons of morning sunlight filter through the office window's closed blinds.

His darting eyes scan the office.

A computer tower hums quietly on an oak desk.

He picks up and reads a brass nameplate.

Doctor Mikel Klinsmann OB/GYN.

The office bathroom door is wide open.

Detweiler freezes, staring at a pair of ankles in slacks jutting out-the wingtip shoes pointing up like skis.

His peek inside makes him glad he missed breakfast.

Doctor Klinsmann lays face up, legs together, arms stretched wide, his unfocused eyes fixed at the ceiling.

Jagged bloody trails trickle from a metal wire wrapped around his throat.

The second body lays face down across his chest. Blood matted hair, shattered bone fragments and brain pulp cover a gaping head wound.

A Sig Sauer compact pistol lies in a congealed pool of blood next to the bodies.

Detweiler unhooks his radio, crouches over them, and spots a bullet hole bored through a ceiling tile.

---

Rocking back and forth on the curb with her knees pulled to her chest, the brunette flinches when Detweiler offers a tissue from his pocket.

"Can you tell me what happened?"

Dabbing her tear puffed cheeks, she sighs without looking up.

"I'm his secretary, when I arrived our security door was unlocked."

"Did doctor Klinsmann forget to lock it?"

"I don't know. He's usually a few minutes late after me."

"There's a red x spray painted on the door. How long has it been there?"

"It wasn't there Friday when I left."

"What did you do next?"

"I knocked and entered his office. The bathroom door was open...I saw his feet...I thought maybe he passed out... that's when..."

She buries her face in her hands, trembling with choked sobs.

⁘⁘⁘⁘⁘

## A WEEK LATER SATURDAY AFTERNOON

A tinkling pentacle door chime announces a visitor.

Frau Horst glances at her watch. Four fifty, ten minutes to closing.

Sniffing fresh spray paint, she bookmarks her page, setting *Life of The Goddess* on the glass counter.

Back turned, his face hidden by a navy-blue hoodie, the visitor lingers at a display carousel of ankhs, birthstones, and amulets.

He doesn't return her friendly "Guten Tag."

"Sir, may I help you?"

He spins around, pulling a gun from his waistband.

Frau Horst gasps, stumbling backward.

Her last memories...his vacant eyes and a blinding flash.

⁘⁘⁘⁘⁘

The visitor drags Frau Horst's body behind the blood-splattered counter, carefully arranging her-face up, arms wide, legs together.

He kneels down and rips her blouse open.

Uncapping a felt tip marker from his pocket he writes a set of numbers on her exposed chest.

He puts the pistol to his temple.

"It is finished…"

He squeezes–the bullet explodes through the left side of his head.

Dead instantly, he drops face down across Frau Horst's body.

The first Monday morning customer finds the bodies.

---

## WEDNESDAY: BAHNHOFSVIERTEL POLIZEI STATION

A fiery oblong sun setting behind hazy motionless clouds turns Frankfurt's skyline a dazzling red.

Alone in his windowless office, Detective Lars Kubach will miss it as usual.

A monotone voice on his office radio delivers Hessischer Rundfunk's top of the hour news headlines.

He yawns and sets aside the crime scene photos and officer Detweiler's notes on his desk.

He stretches, leans back in his chair and closes his eyes.

---

*"A red sharpie was found at the scene. The killer used it to write the numbers twenty-two eighteen under her left breast."*

*Medical Examiner Gerhard Schmidt looks up from the morgue's steel gurney.*

*His gaze locked on Frau Horst's pallid corpse; Lars vigorously scratches his silver brush cut.*

*"Doctor Klinsmann had similar red numbers on his left palm."*

*Schmidt tilts an eyebrow.*

*"Are you suggesting a connection?"*

"It's possible, considering the body arrangements and both killers committing suicide at the scene."

"Perhaps they knew each other?"

"I'm not sure I'm waiting on their background checks…"

---

"Wake up detective."

Lars lifts his head from his folded arms and blinks, trying to focus on the blurred silhouette at his door.

A peaked officer's cap hides Hauptmann Dieter Baumann's receding hairline. A loose-fitting shirt vainly covers his drooping stomach paunch.

He holds up a manila folder.

"Here are the background checks Lars."

"Wunderbar, now we're getting somewhere."

"Are you feeling all right? Your eyes are really red."

"I'm just not sleeping well sir."

"You burn too much midnight oil. Better get some rest. Don't forget my retirement party is Sunday at the *Kaiser Bistro*. Plenty of food and all the Weisen you can drink."

Lars matches Baumann's chubby grin.

"Wouldn't miss it for the world sir."

---

# CHAPTER TWO

A SILENT TELEVISION'S SOFT BLUE FLICKERING light fills the room with dancing shadows.

Six empty Dortmunder Union bottles surround a mustard smeared plate of currywurst remnants on a coffee table.

Face down on his couch Lars snores fitfully.

*"Guten Morgen sir, I am Lars Kubach your new detective."*

*A thinner fuller haired Baumann sets his coffee tumbler down.*

*Lars stands at nervous attention as Baumann reads his file.*

*"Three years as a Bundeswehr MP, third in your academy graduating class, excellent reports from your street years, and you were briefly a semi pro boxer?"*

*Lars eagerly nods.*

*"Hopefully, you will never have to use your fists."*

*Baumann offers a handshake.*

*"Congratulations you are now a member of the team, your area of responsibility is the Bahnhofsviertel."*

*Their first lunch is at Gotz's Bierstube-curled white rindwursts and two beers, Baumann's treat.*

*He flashes an enigmatic smile.*

*"When we finish let's take a trip."*

*Lars, Baumann, and Medical Examiner Bertrand Halmer stand over a steel gurney in Frankfurt's morgue.*

*On Baumann's nod, Halmer lifts the sheet.*

*Lars immediately doubles over and vomits in a bucket on the floor.*

*Baumann and Halmer share matching slivered grins.*

*After a final coughing fit, Lars limply pulls himself up gripping the gurney for support.*

*"Detective, you better learn to block these things. You will see worse I promise."*

*Forcing himself to stare at a half-headed corpse, Lars manages a weak nod.*

*"This man was killed two days ago. Forensics has determined he was shot at close range and the gun placed in his hand. The killer is unknown. This will be your first case."*

---

*A month later, Lars and Baumann clang foamy beer mugs at Gotz's Bierstube.*

*Lars downs a triumphant swallow.*

*"I noticed the victim's refrigerator and cabinets were well organized. According to his family he was not known for such neatness."*

*Lars takes a second gulp.*

*"The victim's cousin has ocd. During my interview with him, I noticed the same organization in his apartment, so I acted on a hunch."*

*"And you were right. We matched fingerprints from two beer bottles in the victim's refrigerator, the cousin confessed when we brought him in."*

*Baumann stands up jingling change in his pocket.*

*Grinning broadly, he inserts coins in an old jukebox.*

*His selection, Beethoven's fifth, keeps playing…and playing…and playing…*

---

Startled awake, Lars blindly fingers the coffee table for his ringing cell phone.

"Kubach here." he mumbles in a gravelly voice.

"Herr Kubach this is Doctor Kolb. I apologize for the early call but it's your brother again."

Yawning, Lars rubs his gritty eyes; his phone screen reads four fourteen.

"What is it?"

"Peter is angry and insists on talking with you."

"Put him on the phone."

Lars hears muffled voices in the background.

"I apologize again sir, but he demands to speak in person."

Lars releases a sharp sigh. "I'm on the way."

Slumped on the couch, he points his remote, clicking off Tagesschau Morgenmagazine.

<hr />

The quiet streetcar glides past rows of dark silhouetted buildings.

Lars stares out the windows at a pink dawn sky casting long shadows on the roofs.

Some riders read newspapers, others listen to headphones, the rest, like him, sit in blank faced silence.

<hr />

*"Peter has severe PTSD. That…and the loss of his left leg has made him violent and suicidal. We recommend that he be permanently admitted." A grim-faced Doctor Gammadi says.*

*Lars gently nudges his frowning mother.*

*"I think it's best for him." He whispers.*

*Doctor Gammadi nods.*

*"Don't worry Frau Kubach he will receive the best care."*

*"I hope so I'm not sure how much more I can take."*

Remembering his mother's haunted face, Lars blinks away a tear as a digital voice announces his stop.

———————— ·+·◆·+·· ————————

## SAINT TIMOTHY KRANKENHAUS MENTAL WARD

The visitor room is pure white-the ceiling, walls, floor tiles, even the flimsy plastic chair that Lars sits in with his knees nearly touching.

A sleepy orderly pushes Peter Kubach's wheelchair in the room and leaves without a word.

"What's the matter Peter?"

"Religion is bullshit."

"Our mother didn't think so."

"What good did her Hail Mary's do me? After praying and kneeling in pews she dies of a stroke."

His face reddening, Lars glares at Peter.

"I didn't come here to debate religion." he says tight lipped.

"Then why are you here?"

"Because you called for me. The doctor says you are uncooperative and refusing your medicine."

Peter snorts.

"They always say that. And big brother is here to see that I behave."

"I understand how you feel."

"No, you don't! You weren't there when the IED blew up our Dingo! The fuckers used an artillery shell! You didn't see my friend's shredded bodies!"

A chubby faced man with severe down's syndrome peeks in the room, mutters to himself and keeps walking.

Leaning forward Peter furiously massages his right knee.

"...the loss of his left leg has made him violent and suicidal."

Peter sighs deeply.

"I'm tired of taking orders from nurses and priests, and idiots who think drugging me is the only answer."

"Life is about taking orders we do it every day."

Peter folds his arms defiantly.

"Well, I'm not anymore."

"Look Peter what do you want? It's almost six I must be at work soon."

"Of course...you might get in trouble for being late."

"It's about dedication!" Lars snaps, "Something you used to have."

"Dedication? Where is my dedicated girlfriend who left me? Or the buddies who promised to visit?"

"I'm here. Look Peter, you did your duty, and you should be proud."

Peter raises his arms in mock worship.

"Oh, I'm proud! Proud that God chose to *test my faith*, by leaving me a cripple, very proud indeed."

"It could have been worse. You could have died."

"And spend eternity burning in hell, some choice."

"Quit blaming God Peter, he did not do this to you."

"He didn't prevent it either. I'm trapped in this fucking wheelchair and this building! I'm drugged and told I can't fit in society! This is my hell!"

Lars glances at the wall clock. The next streetcar arrives in ten minutes. He might catch it if he leaves now.

"Peter, please take your medicine, and give these workers a break I'll talk with them, ok?"

Peter throws up his hands.

"Whatever."

---

"His mood swings are getting worse." An orderly says in the lobby.

Striding briskly, Lars nods, his eyes focused on the exit doors.

"He looks up to you, perhaps you should visit more."

"I will try to make the time."

Arms folded she watches him sprint to catch the arriving Strassenbahn.

# CHAPTER THREE

**THURSDAY MORNING: BAHNHOFSVIERTEL POLIZEI STATION**

SIPPING HIS USUAL BLACK SUGARLESS Jacob's Coffee, Lars scrolls through his computer case notes.

*Victim one: Doctor Mikel Klinsmann, fifty-two, unmarried no children.*

*Licensed OB/GYN with internal medicine PhD from Heidelberg School of Medicine.*

*Opened private practice as a reproductive crisis counselor at the Frauen Helfen Zentrum.*

*No driving offenses, or major debts.*

*Time of death, Friday evening according to medical examiner. Cause of death: Strangulation.*

*Victim two: Angelique Horst, aka Frau Horst.*

*Age forty, owner of Nether Realms new age bookstore.*

*Philosophy degree from Central University Vienna, Austria.*

*Entered Germany on a work visa in the late nineteen nineties.*

*Worked series of odd jobs before opening Nether Realms New Age Bookstore several years ago.*

*Time of death, Saturday evening. Cause of death, gunshot wound to face.*

Lars types in some final notes.

*Neither victim robbed, both killers' young white males.*

*No security videos of the murders, Klinsmann's off, Frau Horst no camera.*

*Recent protests noted at both places*

———————————

After a coffee refill he takes the background checks from his inbox. He reads key points aloud, an old habit.

"Matthias Hinkel, German national age twenty-four. Born in Mannheim. Unstable work history. Current address, unavailable. Fined in 2009 for hashish possession. Social benefits application denied. Both parents killed in vehicle accident January of two thousand five."

Lars pauses. *A horrific accident on Autobahn 5, eight killed, sixteen serious injuries in a thirty-two-car pileup during a raging blizzard that made international news.*

*A relative of Frankfurt's mayor was among the dead.*

He rereads last sentence.

"Admitted to *Saint Timothy Krankenhaus* for severe depression and attempted suicide."

He tents his hands in front of his chin.

"Hmmm…the same hospital as Peter?"

He takes another coffee sip.

"Hans Neubauer, age twenty-five German national, former college student, unknown work history. Lived with parents Joachim and Gertrude. Address, *fifty-one Neuheimer Strasse*, Westend Sud, phone number…"

Lars immediately picks up his office phone.

———————————

## AFTERNOON

Hans Neubauer's parents are well off. Lars secretly envies their spacious living room from a velvet soft microfiber recliner.

A spotless egg white shag carpet, a glass door cabinet displaying rare Hummel figurines, and a giant LCD TV.

Gertrude and Joachim face him on the matching sofa.

Gertrude's cheeks are flushed from crying or fatigue, Lars isn't sure which.

*This is the hardest part of my job.*

"I can't believe he did such a horrible thing. He had such a bright future. Where did we go wrong?"

She shudders and drops her head in Joachim's lap. He tenderly strokes her hair and shoulders.

"I see you are Catholic?" Lars asks, eyeing a giant wall mounted crucifix behind them.

"Yes, and our prayers are for the woman's family." Joachim says.

"I'm Catholic as well and I understand what you are going through." Lars lowers his head. "My mother passed away six months ago."

Gertrude straightens up and dabs her eyes. "We are sorry for your loss Herr Kubach."

"We are willing to cooperate in any way possible Herr Kubach."

"Thank you, sir. You may stop at any time, but I must ask some questions."

Lars opens his notebook and clears his throat.

"Please start with a family profile, anything you wish to say."

Joachim bites off a fingernail; leaning over a glass coffee table he drops it in an overflowing ashtray.

"Do you mind if I smoke?"

"No sir."

Using a gold-plated lighter from his dress shirt pocket Joachim lights a Davidoff cigarillo.

Taking a long draw until the tip glows cherry red, he turns away from Lars to exhale a billowing blue cloud.

He picks up a silver remote, clicking it twice.

A standing Hepa air purifier in the corner instantly hums, pulling the smoke away from a secretly thankful Lars.

"I was a Dresdner Bank global account manager for twenty-five years."

Joachim looks the part; fiftyish, graying brush mustache and hair, worry lines etched in his forehead.

"And my wife is a senior paralegal for the *Kohler and Schmaltz* law firm."

"I've heard of them. Please continue."

"Our son's first passion was soccer he wanted to play for Bayern München."

"I think we all have that dream." Lars says.

Their nervous laughs break the tension.

"But his second love was the church. We hoped he would take up the priesthood."

Smiling at Gertrude, Joachim turns aside to take another puff.

"We paid for his religious studies major at the *Wurzburg Theology School*." He adds.

Gertrude's face suddenly turns grave.

"But his attitude changed in his senior year. He denounced football as the devil's pastime and condemned what he saw as sin everywhere."

Her head lowers, her voice drops to a whisper.

"I must say he became a little troublesome."

"He even criticized my smoking."

Joachim takes a last puff; he grinds the butt in the ashtray–several fall out–his trembling hands put them back.

"Was it the schooling?" Lars asks.

"I don't believe so."

"He did mention attending a church here in Frankfurt." Gertrude interrupts.

"Did he give a name?"

"No but I found a CD in his room. I'll get it."

"Thank you, Frau Neubauer."

Out of earshot, Joachim leans close and whispers.

"She is really crushed by this."

Lars nods sympathetically.

Gertrude hands Lars a CD in a clear case.

"He said a member gave it to him and it inspired him, maybe you can find out how."

"Thank you I will."

"Now about Hans, when was the last time you saw him?"

Gertrude and Joachim exchange thoughtful looks.

"A few days before this tragedy."

"Did he display any unusual behavior?"

"No, he said he was looking for work and spending time with his new church friends."

"Did you meet any of them?"

"No."

Lars tucks his notepad in his dress shirt.

"Before I go there is one last concern."

Joachim lights another cigarillo.

"Go ahead sir."

"I received a call from forensics on my way here. A Walther P38 was found at the scene. It's registered to you Herr Neubauer."

Gertrude gasps and covers her mouth.

Joachim drops his cigarillo scattering glowing ashes on the table, he frantically picks it back up.

"You didn't realize it was missing?" Lars says.

Biting his lip Joachim lowers his head, staring at the carpet he clears his throat.

"My father was a Hauptmann on the Ost front. He shot four Russians during the battle of Kursk. He never used it again the rest of the war. Before he died, he passed it to me. I kept it in my closet, Hans must have taken it his last time here."

Joachim shields his face, his voice cracks.

"And now…it has claimed another life."

Gertrude slides over and gently massages his shoulder.

Lars stands up.

"Thank you for your cooperation during this most difficult time, you have been very helpful. Don't blame yourselves you did all you could as parents."

"Herr Kubach would you like a glass of Riesling before you leave?" Gertrude says.

"No thank you."

He shakes Joachim's hand and hugs Gertrude firmly.

"Oh, I almost forgot, I will need his computer for evidence."

— ◆◆◆◆◆ —

## EVENING: LARS KUBACH'S APARTMENT

Fighting sleep after a ham on rye sandwich and three Dortmunder Unions, Lars listens to a hoarse voice reciting Jonathan Edward's SINNERS IN THE HANDS OF AN ANGRY GOD

He jerks awake between stuttering snores.

*"...They are already bound over to hell..."*

*"...Religion is bullshit."*

*"...Sin is the ruin and misery of the soul..."*

*"...You didn't see my friend's shredded bodies!"*

*"...Your wickedness makes you as heavy as lead..."*

*"...Your damnation does not slumber..."*

*"...and spend eternity burning in hell, some choice."*

The next thing he hears is his alarm.

# CHAPTER FOUR

## FRIDAY: HAUPTMANN BAUMANN'S OFFICE

"I'M CUTTING MY LUNCH SHORT for this."

"My apologies sir, but it's something that couldn't wait."

Lars hands Hauptmann Baumann a tan office mailer.

Baumann clears a stack of papers to one side of his desk and unstrings the mailer.

"I noticed something in the crime scene photos. The murders are remarkably similar." Lars says.

Baumann spreads two photos in front of him. He polishes his reading glasses with a cloth.

"What am I looking at?"

"The numbers on both bodies were done with a red Sharpie. Sixteen twenty on Doctor Klinsmann's left palm and twenty-two eighteen under Frau Horst's left breast."

Baumann peers over his glasses at both pictures.

"I see that."

"And both bodies were carefully arranged postmortem."

Lars pauses as Baumann looks closer.

"Both victims were laid out almost like a cross and the killers shot themselves in such a way as to fall over each victim." Lars says.

"I guess so, rather crudely don't you think?"

"Admittedly yes, but the numbers, and the red x on both doors may have symbolic meanings."

"Hmmm. You may be on to something, and I trust your hunches. You think it might be religious in some way?"

"Matthias Hinkel's social benefits application lists him as Catholic and Hans Neubauer's parents sent him to Catholic Seminary. They said he attended a church and become radical in his beliefs."

"Unless they attended the same church, I don't think that proves a connection."

Baumann hurriedly repacks the mailer.

Lars hides a faint grin.

*He's getting hungry.*

"I admit the killings are similar, so your next step should be to determine if the killers knew each other."

"I'm turning Neubauer's laptop to forensics this afternoon, they should have something in a few days."

"Find out and get back with me. Now let me get moving there's a steak waiting at *Wilhelm's Grill.*"

The Aleenring's rush hour traffic flows around the Hauptbahnhof.

Jammed shoulder to shoulder under a Strassenbahn stop's plexiglass awning, Lars pats his forehead with a hanky.

He spent the scorching afternoon in and out of local stores, each time with the same rehearsed questions.

*"Has anyone bought an unusual number of red sharpies?"*

*"Did you see either of these young men?"*

More stops at Hornbach, OBI and other, smaller hardware stores… more questions…

*"Do you carry Montana Cans brick red spray paint?"*

*"Did you see either of these young men?"*

*Stenmeyer's*, a tiny hobby shop near the train station sold one can to a young man with a backpack and a skateboard-yesterday.

Lars fishes his vibrating cell phone from his slacks.

Holding it away from his sweaty ear, he strains to hear Medical Examiner Schmidt.

"The toxicology reports indicate both killers had high amphetamine levels in their blood."

"What would cause that?" Lars shouts.

The man next to him flashes an irritated glare.

"High levels could be genetic, but certain medicines, and drugs like cocaine can be a factor."

"Could that explain the violence of the murders?"

"It is possible. Some medicinal side effects are aggression and in extreme cases uncontrollable rage, but I have no explanation for these elevated levels."

"Interesting, thank you Herr Schmidt."

Feeling the ground rumble, Lars and the overflow crowd turn their heads and shield their eyes.

The arriving Strassenbahn crawls around a bend through a shimmering heat haze rising from the tracks.

---

Sipping a Dortmunder Union, Lars clicks on Tagesschau's nightly headline news.

*"Now in studio Matthias Stahl reporting."*

*"Guten Abend. Frankfurt-earlier today Polizeipräsident Reinhardt Shurtzmann denied any connection between the recent killings of an abortion doctor and a new age bookstore owner."*

The screen cuts to the Polizeipräsidium press and media room.

Lars sets his bottle down; he clicks his remote raising the volume.

Flanked by high-ranking uniformed officers, Shurtzmann grimly faces flashing cameras and extended arms holding voice recorders.

"At this time, no firm evidence links the two crimes. We believe they are random violent acts. We are still investigating. For now, there will be no further comments."

Barraged by shouted questions, Shurtzmann turns stiffly. The officers protectively follow him out of the room.

Lars clicks the television off.

Chief Baumann's expected phone call comes minutes later.

"He wants to see you Monday morning."

"Most inconvenient since he is on an upper floor."

"You sound drunk."

"I'm just watching a classic denial and diversion technique."

"Quit babbling. Just put together something we can safely release. We don't need the city in a panic just yet."

Lars sighs. "I'm on it chief."

# CHAPTER FIVE

## SATURDAY MORNING

PARTLY HIDDEN BY CHEST HIGH iron rail fences and manicured hedges the box shaped three-story apartments are different only by paint color.

Faint music and singing comes from one of them in the middle of the tree-lined block.

---

Wearing an ankle length purple robe, a slight built rodent faced man with parted silver hair stands behind a cloth covered lectern serving as a pulpit.

His piercing eyes scan the two rows of folding metal chairs packed with anxious men and women.

He raises his arms in a sweeping arc.

The keyboardist, a modest dressed young man with a buzz cut stops playing.

A white-haired usher locks the door and sits on a bench along the back wall.

"Enoch the seventh from Adam was the first prophet…"

A chorus of shouted amens rise from the front row.

"He walked with Jahweh and Jahweh took him. The bible doesn't say much about him, but the Book of Enoch does."

The pastor opens a book on the pulpit.

"Enoch writes that he was visited by the watchers-god's holy angels who warned of a future cataclysm where god would punish the earth with a great destruction!"

The pastor holds up the book, his voice rises.

"The watchers told Enoch to declare that the angels who left their first estate and mingled with the daughters of men should have no peace or forgiveness of sin! In Genesis, angels from heaven impregnated the daughters of men. This unholy union is the true source of our sins! And Jahweh was angry and sent Enoch to warn of his judgement, but they did not listen. So Jahweh destroyed them saving only Noah and his family. Jahweh repented that he made man then. Therefore, he has raised **me**-brother Enoch the second witness to warn the world that he is done repenting!"

Brother Enoch slams his fist on the pulpit, more scattered shouts rise from the front row.

"Our sins have reached to heaven! And like the days of Noah, Jahweh will take vengeance! His judgement of the sinners and ungodly is sure and just and they shall not stand. His sword is upon them!"

Brother Enoch takes a long swallow of bottled mineral water. Clearing his throat, he closes the book.

"There will be a division in the last days. The tares and the wheat have grown together long enough! Enoch warned that Jahweh will come in the clouds with ten thousand of his saints and every work will be tried by flaming fire! And that fateful day will burn as an oven! The wheat will be gathered into the barn and the tares will be gathered and burned! The chaff–the evildoers and God mockers, will be scattered to the four winds! But you…"

Leaning across the pulpit Enoch points his bony index finger at the hushed listeners.

"**You** are the ones chosen to heed Jahweh's holy prophet. **You** are ordained to usher in his kingdom. **You** are holy vessels, gird up your loins and **join him**."

Brother Enoch's eyes flicker upward.

"I send you forth as sheep among wolves. Go and prepare the way of the Lord!"

The keyboardist resumes playing, louder than before.

A woman in the front row yelps. Arms flailing, she bolts up from her chair.

Others stand up raising their arms skyward.

Eyes shut, a man in the second-row mutters and shakes.

Stomping his feet, Brother Enoch leaves the pulpit, joining the frenzied shouting and dancing.

———————— ·+·+·+·+·+· ————————

## AFTERNOON: COMMERZBANK ARENA

Eintracht Frankfurt's last preseason match against FC Nuremburg turned ugly in the second half.

Frankfurt's best midfielder sent off in the 53rd minute…a disputed yellow card in the 68th leading to a converted penalty kick…an 88th minute borderline offside call costing the Eagles a tying goal.

At the final whistle Lars throws up his hands in disgust, joining twenty thousand steady boos filling the Commerzbank Arena.

Adjusting his Frankfurt hat, he leaves his lower bowl seat trudging up the concrete steps.

Sudden shouts and screams come from the next landing.

A panicked crowd disperses leaving two hooligan groups—one in leather jackets—the other in all red locked in a furious brawl of wild haymakers, lunging kicks, shoving, and wrestling.

Lars spots a glinting switchblade; he yells and sprints up the remaining steps.

He never sees the hurtling Jägermeister bottle.

## OSTEND KRANKENHAUS AN HOUR LATER

"You have a grade one concussion mister Kubach, from too much Jägermeister."

His legs dangling off the exam room table, Lars manages a wry smile at Doctor Vigay Rajwal's humor attempt.

"Thanks doc. What are my options?"

Rajwal adjusts his red turban.

"Some rest is needed. I am giving you an anti-inflammatory and a cold compress to place on the knot.

Avoid all stress and activities which may trigger headaches such as computer usage and multitasking."

"Not easy in my line of work, but I do need a rest."

"And mister Kubach," Rajwal points to his temple, "no beer, bad for the blood flow."

"I can't guarantee that."

# CHAPTER SIX

## SUNDAY EVENING

THE *KAISER BISTRO*'S PRIME LOCATION at a four-way intersection offers drinkers and potential johns a street level view of the Bahnhofviertel's red-light district.

Tonight, the drinkers and johns are current and former Polizei officers toasting Hauptmann Baumann's retirement.

"There you are."

Lars grunts from Baumann's drunken backslap.

Gripping a foamy Hefeweizen, he swivels his barstool.

Baumann sways before him in a finely tailored dress uniform despite his girth.

"Nasty golf ball you got there. I see you're drinking to kill the pain. Come meet your new boss." Baumann slurs.

*··◆◆◆◆··*

"Welcome aboard sir." Lars says.

Hauptmann Tobias Muller rises from a booth seat greeting Lars with a firm handshake.

Lars gives him a once over—six feet, flat stomach, squared shoulders, neatly trimmed chestnut hair.

Muller's probing eyes go straight to the knot.

"Thank you. You were at the riot yesterday?"

*Great he already knows.*

"Yes sir, the instigators were *Rot Kommand*, a band of Nuremburg hooligans who pick fights at their matches."

Lips pursed, Muller shakes his head.

"All over a friendly, that's why I stick with racing."

"Our food is here." Baumann interrupts.

Two over-burdened waitresses gratefully set down tall foamy beer glasses and a tray stacked with meat cuts.

---

"I finished training in eighty-eight and spent five years as a patrol officer. During that time, I earned a master's in communication and started climbing the ladder. I'm due for a promotion to Head Inspector one."

Listening to Muller's confident self-appraisal Lars chases two pills with a long sip of Maisel's Weisse.

"So how far do you two go back?" Muller says.

Lars and Baumann share matching grins.

"Do you remember the Bahnhof Patrol scam?" Baumann asks between bites of gravy smothered Jägerschnitzel.

"No, I was stationed in Bonn."

"One of our first cases together."

"Two fake Polizei officers scammed travelers with on-the-spot fines for bogus passport or ticket infractions. They hauled in almost five thousand marks in six-months. For a long time, tourists didn't trust the real police."

Chewing a currywurst, Lars nods in agreement. He sets his fork down to pick up the story.

"They went after easy victims-foreigners, immigrants, tourists. Any protesters were let off with a warning. The fake cops didn't want undue attention."

"How were they caught?"

"After receiving numerous complaints, we launched a sting operation." Baumann answers.

Lars takes a quick sip of beer.

"We set them up with fake tourists. I spent a week undercover in the Hauptbahnhof. The look on their faces was classic when we moved in. Case closed."

Muller cracks a smile. He holds up a foamy glass.

"To a seamless transition."

The trio clang their glasses, taking long swallows.

Lars sucks the lemon wedge and drops it in his empty glass.

Doctor Rajwal was right. Head down, he massages his pounding temples.

Muller taps his shoulder.

"Are you ok?"

"Time to leave sir." he slurs.

"You're not driving, are you?"

"No sir my car is in the shop. I use the Strassenbahn."

Lars renders a drunken salute. He hugs Baumann tightly and staggers to the exit.

Muller nudges Baumann.

"I hope his drinking is not a problem. The media has started focusing on the murders. I need him to have his head right."

"He'll be okay he is just going through a crisis, losing his mom recently and looking after his disabled brother in his spare time." Baumann answers.

# CHAPTER SEVEN

## MONDAY MORNING: POLIZEIPRÄSIDIUM FRANKFURT

SNAPPING A CRISP SALUTE, LARS hands his report to Polizeipräsident Shurtzmann.

Hauptmann Muller sits stone faced in a shiny brown leather armchair.

Standing at ease, Lars watches a pair of clownfish drift back and forth in a soft lit fish tank.

His lime green eyes roam the cherry paneled office, stopping at Shurtzmann's framed pictures and awards.

The former Reserve Luftwaffe Major was also a kickboxing champion.

Shurtzmann closes the folder, his eyes pause at the knot.

*Please don't ask...*

"Your report is very detailed. The weapons were a Walther p thirty-eight and a Sig Sauer compact?"

"Yes sir, the Walther was registered to Herr Neubauer, he was unaware his son took it. The unregistered Sig Sauer was most likely stolen."

"Your report cites protests. Tell me about them."

"Doctor Klinsmann's secretary mentioned a small protest outside his office. A frequent customer of *Nether Realms* stated she had to walk around a protest about a week before Frau Horst's murder. There may be a connection."

"Tenuous at best, we always have protests about something. Do you know if the killers knew each other?"

"No sir, not yet."

"Well then, I stand by my earlier statement. From where I sit it looks the work of random lone nuts."

Shurtzmann folds his arms on his desk. He leans forward, his serious unblinking eyes locking on Lars.

"The press is getting restless. Your answer to all media questions will be 'no comment'. Am I understood?"

"Jawohl, Herr President."

"You are dismissed."

Lars salutes and executes a sharp about face.

In the hallway he gets a text.

*Meet us downstairs.*

---

Part of the Polizei's data research system; the computer forensics detachment is in the basement.

Lars and three technicians; an acne scarred intern, a crew cut supervisor, and Greta—a curvy petite blonde cluster around Hans Neubauer's laptop.

"It was reset to original defaults a week before the murder, but we were able to restore it." Acne scar says with a smug air.

"His emails were encrypted, but we got around that too." Greta adds.

"Seems like he was trying to hide something. What did you find?"

"Surprisingly little, his Facebook account was basic, a blank profile picture, seven friends, and random wall posts—he wasn't on it much." Greta says.

Bent close Lars scribbles the names from Neubauer's friends list in his notepad.

"Unusual for a college kid." He says without looking up.

"His search history was unremarkable. No patterns of conspiracy or antigovernment sites." Acne scar says.

"Did he search for religious websites?"

"Only for college notes it seems." Acne scar says.

"What about his emails?"

"No ranting or antisocial tendencies." crew cut adds.

"Just random college questions about classes, syllabus, and some job applications. Nothing indicates any instability. His last email was months ago."

The other technicians nod in agreement with Greta.

"No porn?"

Lars grins at their blushing faces.

"Now **that's** unusual." He says still grinning.

＋＋＋＋＋＋＋

## ADICKESALLEE U BAHN (SUBWAY)STOP:

A teal-colored U Bahn roars past, trailed by a loud gust of rushing wind.

Lars waits on the subway platform, his phone pressed to one ear, his hand cupped over the other.

"I'm sorry Herr Knapp, could you repeat that?" he shouts.

"I can only tell you that Matthias Hinkel was admitted here in January two thousand six. He was treated by Doctor Victor Kolb."

*Victor Kolb? Peter's doctor?*

"Does doctor Kolb still come in at six?"

"Yes."

"Danke Herr Knapp."

## SAINT TIMOTHY KRANKENHAUS MENTAL WARD

Thin framed, with a shiny balding head and milky complexion, Doctor Kolb is in his mid-fifties.

He strolls with Lars down the empty silent corridor.

Peter's room is the last door on the right.

"What can you tell me about Matthias Hinkel?" Lars asks.

"As you know sir mental health records are kept in the strictest confidence."

"I am aware of that. I'm investigating his involvement in a major crime."

"I see. All I can divulge is that Timothy exhibited suicidal tendencies and thoughts-expected behavior considering he lost both parents. He was treated for chronic depression and given counseling."

"Timothy?" Lars says an eyebrow rising.

"A nickname he insisted on."

"And *you* treated him?"

Doctor Kolb releases a drawn-out sigh.

"Mister Hinkel was released as an outpatient only when it was certain he was well."

"His parents were deceased. Into whose custody was he released?"

"Based on his satisfactory progress his counselor recommended release to a shelter."

"Who provided the counseling?"

"A social worker met him once a week."

"Let me guess, you can't divulge the counselor's or the shelter's name?"

"No sir."

"Were there any follow up appointments?"

"No need, he just had a mental health episode. We all have them at some point in our lives."

"Did he bring up the subject of religion at all?"

"Many of our patients talk about God and religion, some of them have had problems with it in the past."

Peter's room is a few steps away.

"A suicidal young man released without follow up. Based on what happened it seems he didn't get enough help."

"Sometimes Herr Kubach the hurts go deeper than we imagine."

"How is he?" Lars tilts his head to Peter's bed.

Tightly wrapped in a standard thin hospital blanket Peter snores in a curled fetal position.

"He still has outbursts, but he's been better since your visit."

"He looks cold."

"I'll have the nurse bring him a second blanket. In the meantime, he should rest."

Lars quietly closes the door.

"Should I tell him you stopped by?"

"No, I'll be back soon." Lars says over his shoulder.

++++++

## MONDAY EVENING

Three times a week at dusk, Lars jogs on the river walk, an asphalt trail paralleling the river Main.

His route starts and ends at the Westhafen Tower, a cylinder-shaped skyscraper dubbed 'das Gerippte', a wry comparison to its ribbed glass design and an apfelwein glass.

Frankfurt's twinkling financial monuments loom over the river-the Eurotower, Commerzbank, and the Union Investment Building's dazzling blue nighttime façade.

His heartbeat matches the pace of his pounding Nike cross trainers.

Roller-skaters and cyclists flow around him.

Two groups of boys stubbornly play soccer in the fading twilight.

He waves at a strolling couple holding hands.

The distractions are not working.

*"Hello Lars. I have wonderful news. I am getting remarried next Sunday at the Saint Bartholomew Catholic church."*

*"Congratulations Inga I am proud of you."*

*"Thank you. We've been dating for six months. Oscar is funny, articulate, and owns two restaurants in Sachsenhausen—and you know much I like to cook."*

*"I remember. I wish you all the best."*

*An uncomfortable silence passes.*

*"Inga, you know I will always care about you."*

*"I know, Lars I know."*

He slows to a brisk walk-hands on his hips, he stops to stretch his lower back.

He takes a seat on a bench. Under a path light's soft glowing halo, he stares at the city lights mirrored on the Main River's dark surface.

He can't cry.

# CHAPTER EIGHT

A T EXACTLY TWO A.M. JOSHUA Morgan swallows two white, diamond shaped pills with a drink of Rosbacher mineral water.

He turns on his travel radio and lies back on his bed.

*"And the angel cried with a great shout Babylon is fallen that great city who made all nations drink the wine of her fornication. And I the second Enoch cry against the new Babylon of Frankfurt! Let's begin with mammon worship. Nebuchadnezzar built a giant gold statue and commanded that all must bow down and worship it. And what do we see every day, steel and glass towers rising to the heavens! Banks that control the fate of people and nations! We are commanded to bow down and worship them or else starve and live in the gutter!"*

*"Three brave men-Shadrach Meshach and Abednego refused and were sentenced to die in a burning fiery furnace. But Jahweh delivered them! So now we must follow their faithful example and not worship the pillars of mammon, so that we may be delivered as well!"*

*"Jahweh commands us to leave Babylon and forsake her. He will judge Babylon's graven images. He will send a destroying wind and Babylon will sink and be left desolate and those passing by will laugh at her plagues."*

*"Jeremiah the prophet said. 'I have seen your adulteries, and the lewdness of thy whoredom, and the abominations on the hills in the fields.'*
*"Jahweh commands us thou shalt have no other gods before me, yet they served other gods—the sun, the moon, and the hosts of heaven. Judges ten six*

*tells us the children of Israel did evil in the Lord's sight. They forsook him to worship Baal, Tammuz, Diana, Ashtoreth, and Moloch!"*

*"They worshipped the gods of Syria, Zidon, Moab, and the Philistines, instead of almighty Jahweh. They left the lord's house and set up images and groves in every high hill, and under every green tree. The Allah worshippers' mosques with their minarets are the modern-day groves and high places where they commit abominations. Their Imams and leaders keep them in ignorance and darkness under the iron rule of Sharia laws from a murderer who received a visit from a devil. And now they wish to impose the same on the rest of the world!"*

Loud static temporarily interrupts the speaker.

*"Let us go and overturn their graven images and destroy their idols on the high mountains, and hills, and under every green tree and show them the power of almighty Jahweh!"*

*"Just as Noah and the first Enoch warned the world, and as Jonah warned Nineveh, I the second Enoch, warn this generation. We are in the days of the last trumpet. Judgment is left to us. **We** are the reapers sent to eradicate sin! **We** are the avenging angels! **We** are to thrust in the sickle and gather all things that offend and execute judgment. The time has come servants of Jahweh, **we** must surround the walls and sound the trumpet like Joshua! And today is the day."*

Joshua's cell phone chimes a text.

*Today is the day.*

He deletes it and stares blankly at the ceiling.

---

## AFTERNOON: FRANKFURT BAHNHOFSVIERTEL

### *AL ABERRA ISLAMIC CENTER*

A bilingual German and Arabic sign is posted above a storefront office tucked between the *Al Samiyah Kebab Imbiss* and the *Al Hayat* reading room, a converted bookstore with a cracked plate glass window.

Short and stout, sixty-year-old Imam Ali Said's belly protrudes like a mini watermelon under his white thawb.

His full graying beard distracts attention to his balding donut ring hairline.

He is no radical, instead he sends the Islamic Center's students in pairs to the drug dealing Turks and others in trouble with the message to turn to Allah.

On this steamy humid afternoon, he is on his study room phone—and pissed off.

"When are you going to come? They have been outside for an hour now. This is the third time I called."

"I know," the irritated Polizei desk sergeant huffs. "They are conducting a peaceful protest there is nothing we can do–"

"Sorry to interrupt teacher, we chased off one of them trying to spray paint our building."

Jameer, a wispy bearded student stands in the doorway-his head lowered in obvious respect.

Ali Said slams the receiver down.

"Enough of this. Come with me."

Jameer dutifully follows Ali Said past robed barefoot men kneeling face down on prayer rugs.

+ + ✦ ✦ ✦ + +

Hands on his hips, Ali Said glares at a line of men and women silently marching back and forth.

"Where is he?"

"There in the middle."

Jameer points to a scowling man vigorously shaking a spray paint can.

"What are you doing?" Ali Said shouts.

"We are doing God's work." voices yell back.

"Spray painting my center is God's work?"

Nudging Jameer to stay close, Ali Said warily approaches the group.

Still shaking the can, the man steps toward them.

"This is a temple of idolatry. It is a house of devils and must be marked as such." He snarls.

"Who are you to judge another religion?" Ali says.

The sprayer raises his can at Ali Said.

Jameer impulsively slaps it from his hand, it clatters to the pavement.

The sprayer's hard shove sends Jameer stumbling.

Ali Said grabs the wild swinging Jameer by the waist and pulls him away.

Amid louder chants, another protestor hurls the can; it thuds against the Center's door.

The door flings open, two robed men peek out, one yells back inside for help; the other sprints to help Ali Said.

———

Third in line at the Sparkasse Lars answers his phone-frowning at Hauptmann Muller's serious tone.

"Detective Kubach report to the station immediately."

———

## BAHNHOFSVIERTEL POLIZEI STATION

Waiting in the lobby Hauptmann Muller looks up from his wristwatch to Lars.

"A fine keeper of time you are."

"Sorry sir, I was stuck in a long bank line. What's going on?"

"There was a clash between a Christian group and a Muslim prayer room. Two people were injured and eight detained for disorderly conduct."

"How does this involve me?"

"There's one I think you should meet, follow me."

———

Filling a cup at a water cooler, Lars peers through the interview room's one-way glass as Muller narrates.

"His name is Joshua Morgan. He was the main instigator. We did a quick check—he worked at the *Wurst Hutte*, an Imbiss in the Hauptbahnhof."

"Flipping sausages?"

"I guess," Muller shrugs. "Anyway, your report mentioned protests, it's worth an interview."

✦✦✦✦✦

Holding a Styrofoam cup waist high Lars closes the interview room door.

Joshua sits with his arms folded on an oblong metal table.

His short blond hair and defiant granite eyes do not match any of Hans Neubauer's Facebook friends.

"I am detective Lars Kubach. And you are Joshua Morgan?"

"Deuteronomy seven twenty-three says the Lord shall destroy them with a mighty destruction."

"Destroy who?" Lars says after a sip.

"They worship the moon god. We declare Jahweh's judgments on those who worship the hosts of heaven."

"What do you mean we?"

"We are warriors for Jahweh. Second Thessalonians one nine says-"

"Stop." Lars holds up a palm. "This is not a Bible study all I want to know is what happened."

Lars drains his cup; bracing his arms on the table he leans inches from Joshua's face.

"The police report says you tried to deface the Al Aberra Islamic Center."

Joshua smirks and stares straight ahead.

"And Jahweh set a mark upon Cain, lest any finding him should…"

"Enough!"

Lars slams his palms on the table and turns away, the empty cup tips over and rolls to the floor.

A split second later he is inches from Joshua's face.

"I don't want another Bible reference, do you understand! You are facing serious charges young man."

"What charges?" Joshua huffs.

"Assault and battery for starters," Lars snaps. "I want answers. What's the name of the group you were with?"

Joshua maintains his infuriating smirk.

"Have you been at any other protests with this group?"

Joshua shrugs.

"Look young man, I got all day to get answers."

A knock on the door turns their heads.

Hauptmann Muller pokes his face inside, beckoning Lars with his index finger.

Glaring at Joshua Lars slams the door.

⁘ ✦✦✦✦✦ ⁘

"What is it sir?"

"We're going to ticket him for trespassing and release him." Muller says flatly.

"What?" Lars says his face scrunching. "What about the other protesters?"

"They've already been released. This protest led to a near riot. I'm closing this before the media finds out."

"I need to know who these people are."

"Let it go Lars."

"Sir, the police report states he had a spray paint can, and both murder scenes were spray painted."

"Completely unrelated to this."

"Well, I'm not done questioning him."

Muller spins around, face to face with Lars-his hot whispered breath inches from his ear.

"Look let me tell you something," he hisses, "Christians and Muslims rioting in our district? Right now, we don't need more negative publicity. We will dismiss this as a dispute among youths."

"And what do I tell mister Said?" Lars whispers back eyes straight ahead.

"I'm sure you'll think of something." Muller's voice trails as he walks away.

Ali Said briskly strides alongside Lars in the lobby.

"I assure you sir we are innocent; these people were harassing us. My students were only acting to defend me."

"I know sir. But since there was retaliation, we are dropping all charges against both parties."

Ali stops walking and throws up his arms.

"This is crazy!" He shouts and shakes his head.

"I agree sir it's becoming a crazy summer."

Lars yanks open the lobby door and storms out.

## THREE A.M. LARS KUBACH'S APARTMENT

Jolted awake by his ringing cellphone, Lars sits up on his couch, rubs his eyes and yawns.

"Herr Kubach this is Doctor Kolb. I apologize but your brother Peter had another violent nightmare and is currently under supervised watch. We would like to administer Halodan a stronger medicine."

"Do you need my presence?"

"No sir your verbal approval is acceptable."

The phone at his ear, Lars walks sleepily to the toilet.

"Will it help?"

"Yes, he should sleep better once it takes effect."

"Go ahead whatever it takes."

"Thank you, I think it will work just fine for him. I'll keep you posted of any developments."

Call ended; Lars carries an armful of empty beer bottles to his kitchen counter.

# CHAPTER NINE

## WEDNESDAY NINE A.M. BAHNHOFSVIERTEL STATION

A PERSISTENT KNOCK JOLTS LARS FROM his snoring nap.

"Are you ok?" Hauptman Muller eyes him sternly.

"Yes sir, I just haven't been sleeping well."

"Judging by the beer smell oozing from your pores I know why. You need to get it together–the media blizzard has begun despite our best efforts."

He drops a folded newspaper on the desk and walks out.

Lars yawns and unfolds the *Frankfurter Tagblatt*.

* • • • • • *

## POLICE MAINTAIN SILENCE ON KILLINGS

FRANKFURT, – Insisting that the slayings of Doctor Michael Klinsmann and a new age bookstore owner are unrelated, the Polizei have refused further interviews citing privacy concerns.

"We stand by our conclusion that the killings were random violent acts by unstable individuals with no known relationship to each other." A Polizei spokesperson said.

Klinsmann, a well-respected professional was director of the Frauen Helfen Zentrum clinic for unwed mothers and teens. His secretary stated he expressed safety concerns due to a protest the week before his death.

Known simply as Frau Horst, the owner of Nether Realms Bookstore was known for her accurate predictions of love and success. Highly sought after, she was considered a fraud by skeptics. Both victims were slain by young men who committed suicide at the scene.

---

## TWENTY MINUTES LATER

Famous for its ornamental clock, Frankfurt's Hauptbahnhof is an international travel hub and Germany's busiest train station.

Twenty-five platforms, popular fast-food chains, currency exchanges, numerous shops, and food kiosks are all available under its cavernous high arched ceiling.

Lars zigzags through a crowd dispersing from a just arrived regional train.

Stepping around a woman with two impatient children tugging at her waist, he strides to the glass enclosed *Wurst Hutte* at the far end of the station.

---

From a menu of grilled sausages, warm pretzels, watery colas, and beer he selects the American Jumbo-a curled ochre colored sausage smothered with onions, chili, and shredded cheese, stuffed in an undersized bun.

A woman with a ponytail tucked under a green bandana leans out a sliding window with his change.

Lars subtly flashes his badge.

"Are you the owner?"

She nods with a bright smile.

"I am detective Kubach. Do you have an employee named Joshua Morgan?"

She wipes her hands on a grease-stained towel.

"Yes, I remember him."

"You remember him? What happened?"

"He stopped showing up. Umm…about a month ago."

"Was he religious?"

She tilts her head in surprise.

"Yes, how did you know that?"

"I'm a detective."

She laughs.

"He was a little pushy. He handed out tracts and engaged customers in religious debates."

"Do you have any of the tracts?"

She shakes her head.

"Do you know what church he attended?"

Another headshake.

"Do you know where he lives?"

"I'm sorry but I didn't keep his information," She pauses. "Other than that, he seemed like a normal kid."

Without looking, Lars senses a line forming behind him.

"Thank you for your time." He takes a bite of the jumbo. "And the sandwich."

---

**Wednesday evening**

Brother Enoch waits for the usher to admit a visitor with wavy shoulder length hair.

A few heads turn as he quietly sits in the back row.

Enoch clears his throat.

"Isaiah three twelve says women shall rule over them. Romans one twenty-six says God gave them up unto vile affections and a reprobate mind. And who are they that he speaks of?"

"**They**...are of the world therefore **they** speak of the world."

"As it was in Noah's day so shall it be when Jahweh returns! **They** ate and drank, **they** partied and **fornicated with angels!**" And they have corrupted humanity with their **original sin**!

"Jahweh warned the first Enoch he would destroy them and the earth, and Noah obeyed his command to build an ark. As Jahweh's servants we must obey his commands today."

Enoch releases an exaggerated breath; he dabs his sweat beaded forehead with a white hanky. His voice rises to a throaty shout.

"**They** that do such things are worthy of **death**! Jahweh declares that **they** are all **damned** who have pleasure in sin! **And their damnation will not slumber!**"

Enoch takes another deep breath.

"I have one final thing. King Solomon loved many strange women-Moabites, Ammonites, Edomites, and Hittites. Today men of all nations love these strange women of the night. Second Timothy three six says, they creep into houses and lead women into sin!"

"The Eros Houses and saunas lining these very streets serve every sinner who enters their door to hell. But **you**..."

Leaning over the pulpit Enoch points at the clapping and swaying listeners.

"Jahweh has ordained me, the second Enoch to tell the women of this holy house to end this iniquity!"

Enoch raises his arms.

"Leviticus nineteen says do not make thy daughter a whore, lest the land become full of **wickedness**! But that is exactly what is happening here **in our own backyard**!"

"Rise up ye women! Let your voices be heard, show the world that Eve is the pure mother of all creation and women should be worshipped and not be objects of **fleshly lusts!**"

A tall gangly woman bolts up and slaps a tambourine on her wrist. The other women gather around her. Clapping together their voices become a chorus.

"We the daughters of Jahweh and women of Zion come together to bring liberty to the hostage women and girls sold to pleasure wicked men."

One of the women shouts. A man in the front row starts twitching, raising his hands he mutters in tongues.

Enoch passes through the shouting and dancing congregation to greet the visitor waiting in the back.

# CHAPTER TEN

AFTER THREE LITERS OF HEFE Weisen, Lars staggers from the Kaiser Bistro into a muggy twilight.

He stumbles through the *Eros Platz*–the local nickname for the red-light district.

The streets are alive…thumping bass from strip clubs and bars… flashing neon signs…a line of brake lights from drivers gawking at rows of prostitutes.

These are the illegals–East Europeans lured with false job offers, trafficked Africans, and over forty hags making side money to pay rent or support a drug habit.

Sweet tobacco smoke drifts from loitering Turks clustered outside a closed restaurant.

Troublemaking hustlers, they work in pairs, selling sticky thumb sized blocks of hashish or hawking fake watches and other knockoff merchandise.

Lars turns on Rotes Strasse, aptly named for its popular red neon lit brothels-*CUPID HAUS*, *ARTEMIS*, and *LUV PLATZ*.

Briefly tempted by the *Atlantis Spielothek*'s stuttering sign he resists playing slots while drunk.

A dreadlocked man steps in front of him, his open palm flashing a wad of foil packed with black hashish.

"Not interested." Lars slurs.

Brushing rudely past him, Lars darts across Dusseldorfer Strasse to the Hauptbahnhof streetcar stop.

---

Lars is the only rider to exit the near empty streetcar at his Bockenheim stop.

His bleary eyes focus on a billboard featuring a model's airbrushed face.

Schönheit IST hauttief

Beauty IS skin deep.

*Two women are gone from his life–his mother and Inga.*

Sighing, he stumbles the two blocks to his apartment.

---

## THURSDAY: NOON

Shaking his head at the mechanic's claim of hard-to-find parts Lars tosses the overpriced repair receipt on his passenger seat.

A block from the Kaiser Bistro, he slows his 99 Saab for a changing traffic signal.

Across the street, a line of sign carrying women file past the *Eros Sauna*.

The marching women all wear black ankle-length dresses and oxford shoes–a stark contrast to the mini skirted high heeled prostitutes who rule the night.

Lars drives past with one eye on their signs.

*7-27 her house leads to hell!*

*God will judge whoremongers.*

*Flee fornication!*

Two bored Polizei officers monitor the protest from their parked Opel Astra cruiser across the street.

---

Polizei officers Detweiler and Wetzl enter the *Kaiser Bistro* shaking their heads.

Lars turns his barstool from Sky Sports TV to watch the women file past the bar's large window.

"What's that all about?" he asks Detweiler.

"Some women's rights group, they say their mission is to cleanse this area of prostitution."

"Good luck." Lars says with a sarcastic grin.

"Right," Wetzl smirks. "They were at the Frauen Helfen Zentrum a few weeks ago too."

"This is the same group?"

"Yes, they are a bunch of kooks."

Lars gulps down his Apfelwein shot. Leaving a half finished currywurst he darts outside past the officers and bartender's puzzled faces.

---

A reporter with frizzy cinnamon hair holds up a voice recorder to a tall rail thin apple cheeked protestor.

"We are Jahweh's daughters, and he has washed our filth." She says proudly.

Comparing her to a stork, Lars drifts past, lingering by a pizzeria shop window.

"And why are you protesting?" Frizzy hair asks.

"We are here to stop men from exploiting women when they should be home with their wives."

Frizzy hair follows her shifting eyes; Lars turns his face-too late.

Matching his brisk pace, frizzy hair thrusts his voice recorder toward Lars.

"May I speak with you sir?"

Lars shakes his head.

"Is this part of your investigation?"

"No comment." Lars grunts.

"Are there any leads in the recent killings?"

"No comment."

Brushing past frizzy hair, Lars slams his car door- tires squealing, he zips from the curb to the intersection.

"You got that didn't you?" Frizzy hair says to his nodding cameraman.

---

## TWO A.M. SHORTWAVE BROADCAST

*"Woe to them that devise iniquity and work evil on their beds! Woe to the corrupt bloody city, full of lies and robberies! Every day bright lights and sensuous pleasures seduce sinful men. Ezekiel says they gave gifts to all whores. But Jahweh's word says God forbid that the members of Christ should be with a harlot."*

*"You adulterers are friends of the world and enemies of God. Your bodies are the* members of God, *not prostitutes. He that joins with a harlot partakes of her sins and absorbs her demons because two says Jahweh shall be one flesh."*

*"God will judge whoremongers and adulterers. Those who sow to the flesh shall reap corruption. Cleanse your hands, ye sinners and purify your hearts ye double minded."*

*"Proverbs warns us not to follow her ways and her house is the way to hell leading to the **chambers of death!**"*

*"Pharoah's wife imprisoned Joseph, and Salome had John the Baptist executed because they stood for purity in this corrupted sinful world. And like them we must be willing take a stand and to give our lives."*

*"O harlot hear the word of the Lord. The time has come to cast you from your pleasure house. You shall cease to be a harlot for men who enter your house of sin for a season."*

*"She that lives in pleasure is dead while she lives and will be punished for her lewdness and whoredoms."*

*"Because of your whoredom and witchcraft Jahweh says I will make you stop playing the harlot. And just as he allowed the dogs to feast on Jezebel's dead body, your house will burn with fire and your judgment will be in*

*the sight of **many women**! I say again, her house is the way to hell leading to the **chambers of death!**"*

Brushing his mane of greasy hair from his face the listener turns off his radio.

Feeling lightheaded, he sits down in his dark apartment, trembling at the returning vision-a swirling bloody kaleidoscope and a woman's spectral mutilated face.

# CHAPTER ELEVEN

## Friday: Six thirty A.M.

Holding his coffee mug waist high, Lars paces his living room listening to Hauptmann Muller's series of voicemails on speakerphone.

4:18 A.M. *"There's been another murder. Call me as soon as you get this."*

4:24 *"Detective Kubach pick up."*

4:30 *"Lars this is urgent call me asap."*

4:50 *"Before you do anything else today meet me in my office."*

---

## Bahnhofsviertel Polizei Station: Seven A.M.

Hauptmann Muller paces behind his desk, sighing and shaking his head.

Hands on his hips, he turns-glaring at Lars.

"What the hell's wrong with your phone?"

"My head was killing me, so I shut it off."

"Did you see the news this morning?"

"No sir."

"I did, and so did most of Frankfurt. ZDF morning magazine released a video of you and that *Tagblatt* reporter."

Lars rolls his eyes.

"He was badgering me with questions."

"You did all right until you sped off like a bat out of hell. What message do you think that sends to viewers? That we have a hot head detective on the case?"

"Of course, they used the worst possible footage. And besides, I wanted to test my car since I just got it back."

"Now listen to me! Shurtzmann has been riding my ass about the rising crime in our district. We don't need that hotshot reporter pouncing on the slightest reason to sensationalize the latest murder. Here, take this."

"A business card?"

"The address of the murder."

"I saw a woman's group protesting there yesterday." Lars says guardedly.

Muller waves a dismissive hand.

"Let's not draw conclusions yet. Keep what you find secret until we can figure out what the hell's going on. And another thing. Keep your damn phone on too."


## BAHNHOFSVIERTEL: RED LIGHT DISTRICT 8:00 A.M.

Formerly known as the *Venus Erotik*, the *Eros Sauna* is a five story "hostel" famous for its pink neon lit windows and a busty woman's flashing neon outline above the door.

The website describes it as "*an upscale appointment only massage parlor...*" but Lars knows better–the six women featured on the home page are legally licensed–the rest working the upstairs rooms are not.

Frau Mecklenburg–the owner and a well-known socialite is the apparent victim.

An obvious prostitute in a halter top and skin-tight leather shorts struts past Lars taking snapshots of a red x on the door.

He presses the intercom.

"Who is it?" a high-pitched accented voice says.

"Detective Lars Kubach. I am here to see Oom."

"I already answer questions."

"I have been assigned to investigate Frau Mecklenburg's murder."

———————— ·+✦✦✦+· ————————

Inhaling perfume and incense Lars enters a shiny black marble floored lobby with rose painted walls.

A flashing pink neon MASSAGE sign points to a marble stairwell. A second red BAR sign blinks above a thick curtained doorway.

Oom sits cross legged on the lobby's red velvet sectional couch.

Her bronze skinned petite frame, pouty lips, and straight black shoulder length hair make her the most requested masseuse.

"Are you the co-owner?"

Her slanted half-moon eyes red from tears, Oom nods.

Lars points to the BAR sign.

"How about I have a few drinks and we talk?"

———————— ·+✦✦✦+· ————————

Lars sits on a four-legged barstool waiting for the foam to settle in his ten Euro glass of Dortmunder Union.

Behind the L shaped counter Oom pours a Fanta in an ice cube filled glass.

The dimly lit bar is empty, but Lars knows the game-during "business hours" bikini clad working girls wait to swarm customers with offers of "courtesy drinks" or a "massage."

"Were you working last night?" Lars asks.

"No, I work daytime."

"Tell me what happened."

Oom sighs. "Girls call me for emergency. When I come in police already here. They ask rapid questions we in shock not know what to say."

"Continue please."

"And a TV truck with cameras comes too."

"The media was here so quickly?"

Oom nods. "Police make them stay outside."

"Can I interview the workers?"

"Police boss already interview. He made me send them home. I am only one here. I wait for crime scene cleanup to show up."

"Who asked the questions?"

"Tall man..." Oom stretches one arm high over her head, "Brown hair—mean eyes."

"Did he see the body?"

Oom nods vigorously.

"He searches room I not allowed inside until coroner comes."

Lars points to crime scene tape stretched over a door marked PRIVAT.

"I want to look inside."

—————————————✦✦✦✦✦—————————————

*The murder was quick—and violent...*

Hands clasped behind his back, Lars studies a wild pattern of bloody shoeprints and a blood-spattered massage table tipped over in a corner.

In the doorway Oom sniffles and rubs her tearing eyes.

"Were there any witnesses?"

"No, two girls hear a gun shoot and find the bodies."

"I saw the lobby ceiling camera, that should have something."

"I tell police it's not working."

"You lied to them?" Lars looks at her sternly.

Oom shrugs her bony shoulders.

"I don't like the tall man he acts mean to the girls, yelling at police to search rooms, and say I am in trouble for illegal workers."

"I'm not here to bust you I just need to review the footage for clues."

---

## Mid-afternoon: Lars Kubach's Office

Lars fast forwards the silent grainy DVR footage to the approximate time of the murder.

At three seventeen a.m. Frau Mecklenburg relaxes on the lobby couch trimming her cuticles.

Sipping coffee, Lars studies her silver hair pulled back in a tight bun, hula hoop earrings, and excessive makeup to hide her true age.

She looks up suddenly and crosses the lobby.

She lets in a visitor wearing a backward ball cap, surplus digital Bundeswehr fatigues, and a backpack slung over one shoulder; he follows her to the couch.

They talk for a minute and twelve seconds.

Frame by frame Lars examines his pockmarked face and blonde hair sticking out under his hat.

At three twenty Frau Mecklenburg smiles and leads him by the hand to the bar.

From three twenty-two to three thirty-nine the surveillance footage records the empty lobby.

At three forty, two girls in high heels and bikinis rush down the stairwell and urgently stutter step across the lobby to the bar.

A minute later one of them stumbles through the curtain with her hands over her mouth.

The other girl frantically paces the lobby making multiple phone calls.

---

# FRANKFURT MORGUE

Arms tightly crossed, Lars shivers waiting for coroner Schmidt to slide out two metal gurneys.

Schmidt pulls back the white sheet covering Frau Mecklenburg's battered face.

He looks sideways at Lars; his hands are tented over his mouth.

*"You better learn to block these things you will see worse I promise."*

"A claw hammer was found in the room. It looks like he choked her out first probably from behind." Schmidt says.

"That would explain the lack of screams or sounds of struggle."

Schmidt nods somberly.

"And the knocked over table as she fell. The killer struck her multiple times then shot himself with a PMR-thirty Kel Tec. The victim was arranged like the previous two. I think you know what else I found."

"More numbers?"

"Yes, seven two seven in red marker above her navel, this time there is something else as well."

Schmidt lifts the killer's stiffened arm.

"Under the armpit."

Ignoring the bullet shattered skull, Lars bends close rubbing his chin and squinting at two tiny letters.

"A JW tattoo? Could it be his initials?"

"I'm not sure, I don't have an id yet."

"Check the other killers for the same tattoo."

"Sure, I'll contact you as soon as I do."

"Thank you. One last thing. Do not release any details to the media. We don't need unfounded conspiracies."

## Late Friday Evening: Bahnhofsviertel Station

Hauptmann Muller shuffles through the crime scene photos while Lars narrates as if reading a script.

"Her name is Gabrielle Mecklenburg age fifty-nine. She started as an exotic dancer and bought the old *Venus Erotik*. No known enemies or dissatisfied clients."

"Anything else?"

"I checked–the Kel Tec is unregistered."

"Of course." Eyes closed Muller shakes his head.

"Sir…" Lars pauses, "this one is just like the others, the violence, the body arrangement, strange protests…"

"I know, I know," Muller nervously rubs his fresh haircut, "what about the killer?"

"The DVR didn't give me much. Just before closing time Frau Mecklenburg lets him in, they talk briefly, then she takes him to the bar where she had a private room. I compared his face to Neubauer's Facebook friends-no matches."

"And how did *you* get video footage? What's her name-Oom? She said the DVR wasn't working."

"So, you *were* at the scene?" Lars says accusingly.

"Well, I certainly couldn't wait for you to shake off another hangover. You will surrender it to forensics. They will work on it over the weekend."

"Yes sir…right away." Lars says through clenched teeth.

# CHAPTER TWELVE

**SUNDAY MORNING**

RUMBLING THUNDER ECHOES IN THE distance.
Warily eyeing an approaching band of ominous purple clouds, Lars zips up his Jack Wolfskin jacket.

Scattered rain drops pelt his umbrella as he strolls down a shiny cobblestone path lined with dripping wet plants.

The Palmengarten, Frankfurt's famous botanical garden is deserted this Sunday morning leaving him alone to think.

*Yesterday he browsed the Schaumainkai flea market-his only purchase, a Volksmusik CD with a white bearded potbellied man in Lederhosen, a checkered shirt, and a green alpine hat on the cover.*

*His interviews with local tattoo artists yielded nothing; nobody remembered a JW tattoo under an armpit.*

*"That takes guts," one artist said, "I would remember that."*

*His day ended at the Kaiser Bistro, frowning over Eintracht Frankfurt's 4-0 season opener loss.*

———◆◆◆◆◆———

A clinging mist shrouds a hedge lined well-manicured emerald-green courtyard.

Through steady rain dripping from his umbrella rim Lars stares at the flower beds of white lilies, blue Siberian irises, and lavender peonies.

Inga loved this spot, they often held hands as she compared flower colors.

He lifts up his jacket sleeve checking a glittering wristwatch, her first anniversary gift to him.

He sighs-in a few hours she will be officially remarried.

---

## FRANKURT MADAM HAD BLACK BOOK

Bahnhofsviertel. – Gabrielle Mecklenburg, the *Eros Sauna's* slain owner allegedly kept a private visitor log. Employees said she recorded names of high-profile customers based on services performed and length of visit.

Catering to upscale clients, the famous massage parlor has been targeted by complaints and a recent protest from a women's rights group.

An unidentified male bludgeoned Frau Mecklenburg to death before committing suicide.

The brutal crime is the third in two months. A renowned abortion doctor and a new age bookstore owner were slain by young men who killed themselves afterward. Despite similarities the Polizei steadfastly deny any connection.

---

Lars folds the *Frankfurter Tagblatt.*

Taking measured sips of steaming black Jacob's Coffee, he stares out the *Garten Café's* rain-streaked windows.

He finally makes the phone call.

---

## AFTERNOON: THE KAISER BISTRO

Faces turn at the sound of Oom's flapping sandals.

Her skin-tight black yoga pants and stomach revealing shirt draw furtive stares from the Kaiser Bistro's afternoon drinkers.

Lars is one of them–he drains a Maisel's Weisse and motions her to join him at the bar.

Straddling a stool, she peers into his bloodshot eyes.

"You are drunk so early?"

He shrugs.

"I called about your special." He slurs.

"You want massage? Plenty girls for you to pick but Sauna still closed, only I can go inside."

"I want you," he says with a lusting grin, "but cash only no credit card."

Oom shakes her head. "Extra without card."

"How much?"

"Two hundred Euros."

Lars flips through a knot of notes in his wallet.

"How about one hundred and I pay for a room?"

Oom rolls her eyes, brushing away a hair strand she frowns at him with tightly pursed lips.

"Ok, but only this time."

The same bar faces jealously follow them to the exit.

———— ·•••••· ————

## *HOTEL DER FRANKFURTER*

Laying bare-chested on a king-sized bed Lars admires a full color Bengal tiger tattoo covering Oom's lower back.

"How did you become the Eros Sauna co-owner?"

"I start as Frau M's maid. She teaches me German then promotes me making me in charge of daytime workers."

Her hands glistening with baby oil, Oom turns around.

"Roll over now."

He grunts sharply as her fingers knead his shoulder blades like warm dough.

"What else do you know about her?"

"She have lot of money and owns *big* house."

Oom emphasizes by spreading her arms wide.

"No married, no boyfriend, just have two cats."

"The Tagblatt said she kept a visitor log, do you, have it?"

"Missing, reporter interview my workers, maybe one of them tell him by mistake."

"A red-haired reporter?"

"Yes, you know him?"

"He seems to know me."

"Roll on your side now."

Oom grins and casually brushes the growing bulge under his white towel.

"Looks like time for special."

———— ⋅⋅✦✦⋅⋅ ————

## Two hours later

*Positive id on killer. See us 1ˢᵗ thing Monday.*

Careful not to wake Oom, Lars gingerly sets his cell phone back on the hotel nightstand.

Draping his arm over her, he falls asleep smiling.

# CHAPTER THIRTEEN

**MONDAY MORNING: POLIZEIPRÄSIDIUM EVIDENCE LAB**

TWO TECHNICIANS IN BLUE LAB coats greet Lars with handshakes.
"Guten Morgen detective Kubach I'm Jorge Stielhausner and this is
my assistant Franc Behr. Come with us."

The technicians are an odd couple-Stielhausner, weary and rugged
faced with a stooped walk, and Behr, a lanky energetic trainee.

Lars silently dubs them veteran and rookie.

They pass cubicles of workers facing computer screens, shuffling
through document piles, or chatting on phones.

⋅⁺◆◆◆◆⁺⋅

Bent close, Lars watches a much clearer digitally enhanced version
of the Eros Sauna security footage.

The veteran isolates and magnifies the killer's face.

"We ran fingerprints from the hammer and a spray can in his
backpack. Your security video confirmed his identity."

"His name is Detlef Bergmeyer, German national age twenty. He
was in the Polizei databank for shoplifting at Galleria Kaufhof earlier
this year." Rookie adds.

Lars studies the face.

"Was the spray can from Montana Cans?"

"Yes, the color is brick red, a match to the x on the door." Rookie answers.

"What else was in his backpack?"

"Not much–loose change, deodorant, and a set of keys."

"No religious items like tracts or CDs?"

Veteran and rookie share puzzled looks.

"No sir." They answer together.

. ⁘ .

# ELEVEN A.M.

Detlef Bergmeyer's police file lists his address as a room above *Schweitzer's Bierstube*, on Moselstrasse.

Ducking under a swaying light bulb, Lars follows the heavyset bar owner up a flight of skinny creaky stairs.

"Don't know much about the kid, but he scraped up rent every month. Around here we don't ask how if you know what I mean."

"I get it."

Lars hands him Detlef's key.

Stooped over the lock, the owner's chubby fingers twist the key until the lock clicks.

"Ahh there you go." He grunts.

A strong musty odor escapes from the open door.

Together they stand, with hands over their mouths.

His face pinched in disgust, the owner fans it away.

"Just lock it and return the key to the bar when you finish."

"Thank you, sir, I won't be long."

Lars presses the light switch; a low watt bare ceiling bulb pops on.

A roach skitters across the wood floor, disappearing under a baseboard.

Straddling a pile of clothes, Lars pulls a ceiling fan chain.

The motor hums, the ticking blades slowly rotate.

The furniture is second hand-a foldaway sofa bed, a peeling fake wood table, and a recliner with orange foam bulging from a split cushion.

A silver shortwave radio rests on top of a heavily scratched dresser.

The station is preset to 3955.

He presses it…nothing but static and garbled voices.

Working the stubborn top drawer open he sorts through a pile of video games-*Slaughter Haus Cannibals, Zombie Invaders, Killer Carnival Clowns*.

The second drawer opens easier.

Inside, a game controller, pens, an *Inuus Lauf Haus* business card, and…a notebook with blank pages.

Tucked inside is an old paystub, and Detlef's Personalausweis.

"He left his id?"

Lars pockets the plastic card and picks up a religious tract with a stylized cross on the cover.

He thumbs through *Sin and the Human Condition* stopping at a Bible verse underlined in bold red.

*For every battle of the warrior is with confused noise, and garments rolled in blood…*

He casually picks up an empty prescription bottle.

"Halodan? The same drug Peter is now taking, hmmm."

The prescription was filled two weeks ago.

"Wait a minute."

His eyes stinging from sweat, he pulls apart a pair of gaudy checkered drapes.

Dazzling sunlight floods the room through a smudged cracked window.

Using the better light, he brings the bottle closer, squinting to make sure.

"Prescribed by Doctor Victor Kolb?"

He pulls his phone from his pocket.

*Guten tag Herr Schmidt, detective Kubach. I am requesting a second blood test for each killer. I am looking for traces of a drug called Halodan.*

Text message sent; he shields his eyes peering over a ledge spattered with pigeon droppings.

The culprits are perched on the ledge directly above.

He flips through the tract again, stopping at the underlined verse.

Joshua Morgan's snarling comment comes back.

"*We are warriors for Jahweh…*"

"Wait a minute! J…W…the tattoos…"

He snaps his fingers.

"That's it! J W must be Jahweh's Warriors!"

---

Pouring sweat from the rain forest heat, Lars sets the Saab's air-conditioning to max.

Grinning widely, he deliberately swerves, scattering a flock of strutting pigeons.

# CHAPTER FOURTEEN

## Bahnhofsviertel: Three P.M.

A ROW OF EUROPEAN UNION MEMBER flags flutter over the *Der Frankfurter* entrance.

The recently renovated hotel borders the red-light district.

Its marble façade, and glistening onyx tiled lobby are prominently displayed on the 'four stars' hotel's website and brochures.

The surrounding neighborhood is a different story.

At *Fung Lun's Nudel Haus* customers can choose from a variety of noodle dishes made by the ancient, stooped patriarch and his family.

The *Instanbul Palace* is great for a two a.m. Doner Kebab if you don't mind the whispered "hashish, hashish" from the Turk drug sellers lingering outside.

Next door is *LA GIRLS*, a strip club stocked with bronze tanned, buxom blonde dancers.

At the end of the block is *Horney's Irish Pub*.

Expat Graham Sweetham, a former English rugby player is the owner. A towering six five, two sixty, he retired from back injuries after four years with London's Harlequins.

Years ago, African immigrants ran a vast hashish smuggling network along with the ever present Turkish 'baba's heroin trade; in the nineties they grudgingly shared turf when the Russian *Mafiya* muscled in with Eastern bloc trafficked women.

The latest problem is Balkan gangs. They run illegal gambling dens and protection rackets extorting the red-light district's fruit market and clothing vendors.

There have been occasional flare-ups.

Lars smiles, he knows the area **so** well.

A friendly silver haired white gloved doorman in a maroon uniform holds the heavy glass door open for him.

Remembering his night with Oom Lars stifles a grin at the bilingual sign on the admissions desk.

*Nein Prostitution Kunden strikt durchgesetzt*

*No prostitution customers strictly enforced.*

"Back again sir?"

Ignoring the clean-shaven desk clerk's annoying smirk, Lars sounds official as he flashes his badge.

"Mister Von Schaub is expecting me."

His smirk vanishing, the clerk points to an elevator.

"Second floor, first room on the right sir."

---

Otto Von Schaub is impeccably dressed, creased Tommy Hilfiger slacks, Louis Vuitton loafers, and a dress shirt with a Hugo Boss tie.

Despite the heat he wears the hotel's maroon vest.

His thatch of white hair, wrinkled cheeks, and expressive eyebrows give him a wizardly look.

Lars accepts his handshake and sinks into a genuine leather recliner.

Von Schaub unlocks the bottom drawer of his massive oak desk.

"I dug up his records as you asked. Here they are."

Lars thumbs through two months of Detlef's pay stubs.

*The pay address—Schweitzer's Bierstube.*

"What can you tell me about him?"

"He was a good porter, but he seemed distant. He was so unsociable to visitors we finally let him go."

"Was he religious?"

"Not that I'm aware, as I said he never talked much."

"Did he have a prior work history?"

"He worked three months as a Lufthansa baggage handler. I thought the experience would be useful since we sometimes get foreign travelers with many bags. He looked like he was up to it."

"I'm asking Herr Schaub, because Detlef is a crime suspect, the media hasn't found out yet. If you wish to avoid scrutiny, keep his employment here a secret. I will do the same."

Von Schaub gratefully nods.

"No problem we have enough issues around here."

---

## BAHNHOFSVIERTEL: RED LIGHT DISTRICT

The *Inuus Lauf Haus* is a five-story brothel recognizable by its red heart shaped neon lights.

Parked outside Lars punches the business card number in his phone.

Years ago, an enraged drunken G.I. in transit from Iraq assaulted a Korean sex worker on the third floor. He disarmed and shot a Polizei officer; after a bullet filled street chase, he was shot several times and died in an alley.

The local and foreign media covered up the incident as a botched robbery.

The Korean prostitute was quietly deported.

Assigned to the case due to his excellent English, Lars translated the tragedy to the American military police.

He slides his phone back in his pocket.

The 'manager' has agreed to meet him on the second floor in ten minutes.

---

A ruby red flashing arrow points to a curving hallway leading upstairs.

Trudging up a flight of narrow wooden stairs well-worn from years of foot traffic, Lars casually reads graffiti on the red ceramic tiled walls.

*Nerds Unite*

*Spartacus was here*

*It's all pink inside*

The graffiti artist's warped humor was right-the second-floor hallway's walls and floor tiles are all hot pink.

Glowing cherry red fluorescent tubes line the ceiling.

His face scrunched from the overwhelming perfume, Lars strides past a dozen open doors, ignoring leering glances and whispers to "come inside."

Some women sit cross legged on stools, their bikinis glowing under blacklights, others lay seductively in beds framed with blinking rope lights.

The Door's *Light My Fire* blares from the last room at the end of the hall.

Hit by a sudden nauseating wave of body odor, Lars peeks inside.

He has never seen someone so obese.

Wearing only checkered boxer shorts, the manager sits on a bed with two girls in bikinis.

His bloated white belly jiggles as he reaches to turn off the radio.

He shoos the secretly grateful girls from the bed, they brush past Lars with relieved smiles.

"Now what did you want?" The owner says with a labored grunt.

"I believe this young man worked here."

His lips pursed tightly, Lars hands him Detlef's Personalausweis.

"Yeah, I remember him, pretty strange kid."

———— ·+++++· ————

Thirty minutes later Lars is on his phone with Lufthansa hiring coordinator Ulf Lloris.

"You hired Detlef through a temporary service?"

"Yes, originally as a baggage handler. He also cleaned the terminals vacuuming carpets, washing windows, emptying garbage."

"Why was he fired?"

"He kept harassing one of our ticket clerks. She was Muslim, you know the scarf, long skirt all that."

"What did he do...? Oh Scheisse!"

Lars slams his brakes; he glares at the pedestrian darting in front of him.

"I'm sorry Herr Lloris, please continue."

"He called her names under his breath and made rude comments."

"Do you think her religion had anything to do with it?"

"Yes, in fact he left a Bible tract on her counter called *The Real Infidels*. She was so upset we fired him."

"Do you still have it?"

"No sir this was some months ago."

"May I speak with her?"

"I'm sorry Herr Kubach but she quit recently."

"Thank you for your cooperation, Herr Lloris."

# CHAPTER FIFTEEN

"DETLEF BERGMEYER'S FATHER WAS A dock worker in Hamburg and was never home. After his parents divorced, his mother moved here and turned to heroin leaving him to fend for himself. By fifteen he was on the streets."

Fingers laced behind his head Hauptman Muller leans back in his chair.

"A rough childhood, continue Lars."

"He rented a room at an illegal Gasthaus for transients and prostitutes."

Muller purses his lips and looks at the ceiling.

"He cleaned rooms and peep show booths at *Inuus Lauf House*. The manager..." Lars uses air quotes. "Felt sorry for him and offered him the job."

"Better than nothing I guess." Muller says with a disgusted shudder.

"He had an argument and called one of the workers a whore. Security escorted him out and he never returned."

"Continue Lars."

"Lufthansa fired him for harassing a Muslim worker. His last known job was a porter at the *Der Frankfurter*. Except for a minor shoplifting charge, he dropped out of sight."

"And then he resurfaces and kills a madam in cold blood. His lingering bitterness against women stemmed from his childhood. That-his aimless life, and addiction to violent videogames, led him to kill."

"You sound like a lawyer sir."

"A reporter from the fucking *Tagblatt* is due to interview me before lunch. I need a possible motive."

---

## LARS KUBACH'S OFFICE

Sipping coffee Lars skims Wikipedia's brief description of Jahweh's Warriors.

*Jahweh's Warriors is a fringe religious group founded by a former drug dealer and self-proclaimed prophet known as Brother Enoch. The group's beliefs are loosely based on the writings of John Rushdooney and Francis Schaeffer, strong proponents of Dominion theology which teaches that Biblical instead of secular laws should be used as standards to govern society. Brother Enoch insists his mission is to implement such laws.*

*His apocalyptic end time scenario claims he will lead a remnant ordained by God to punish the world.*

*He hosts a nightly shortwave broadcast. The group does not have a website or email contact.*

Lars clicks a link in the notes section.

The German website, *www.sectwatch.org/archivs*, opens with a crimson full moon rising behind a screen of skeletal leafless trees.

---

### CHECKERED PAST MAKES PREACHER'S PROPHECIES SUSPECT.

**Self-appointed prophet teaches a gospel of fear and a bible dominated society.**

*Wilhelm Kugel aka Brother Enoch the charismatic leader and founder of the apocalyptic Jahweh's Warriors has a most unchristian past. His half hour rants against abortion, gay rights, and government conspiracies are broadcast daily on shortwave at 2 a.m.*

*Born in 1959 to a German mother and American soldier father he spent his childhood in Detroit Michigan.*

*Abandoned by the abusive father, Kugel's mother returned to Germany and became a street prostitute working from a car in the infamous 'forty-mark parks' so prevalent in the seventies and eighties.*

*She died of an undisclosed illness in 1988.*

*Little else is known about Kugel until his 2004 arrest for opium possession and pimping.*

*During his incarceration he renounced his former hippy and drug dealer life and formed a small prison chapel ministry. His original sentence of two years was reduced to six months.*

*Upon his release he became an itinerant street corner preacher and joined a variety of fringe sects often leaving over doctrinal disagreements. After his most recent split from the Latter Rain Baptist Tabernacle, he preached in Frankfurt's Bahnhofsviertel.*

*With monetary support from a core group of followers he received enough donations to start a radio ministry.*

*Jahweh's warriors claim about twenty members and are nomadic without a known fixed address. Despite their end time views that they will carry out God's judgments before his millennial reign, the sect is not considered a threat to social order. Brother Enoch's shortwave broadcast may be using a pirated signal.*

Article saved; Lars grabs his keys—the closest Media Markt closes in thirty minutes.


## TUESDAY EVENING: BAHNHOFSVIERTEL


After an hour spent losing eighty Euros on a video slot machine, Lars leaves the *Platinum Spielothek*.

In the humid twilight he strolls down Moselstrasse, looking for something to eat-ignoring *DIVA'S* pushy doorman handing out flyers for the club's private upstairs table dance shows.

Next door is *CUPID'S,* a brothel famous for its trademark neon outlined cherub wearing only an arrow filled quiver.

Sizzling meat, pungent spices, and grilled onions waft out *Tuncay's Kebap's* open sliding glass window.

Inside, wailing Arabic music blares from a battered radio with a bent antenna.

Amid rising smoke from a steaming flat grill, two swarthy men in aprons hurriedly take orders, a third shaves thin slices of lamb meat from a rotating inverted cone.

Reading the *Frankfurter TagBlatt,* Lars waits for his order-a glass of Maisel's Weisse and the Ottoman; three lamb skewers with fresh grilled tomatoes, peppers, onions, and a side of rice pilaf.

Feeling eyes on him he lowers the paper; a curious toddler stopped at his table silently stares up at him.

The boy's mother, a petite woman wearing a green Abaya and matching hijab takes the boy's arm.

"So sorry sir." She says softly.

Lars smiles and hands the boy a two Euro coin.

His smile vanishes at the second page headline.

---

## DID VIOLENT VIDEO GAMES LEAD TO MADAM'S KILLING?

*FRANKFRUT – Socialite Frau Mecklenburg's slaying may have resulted from an obsession with violent video games found in the alleged killer's apartment.*

*According to the owner of Schweitzer's Bierstube he lived alone in a one room upstairs rental.*

*"I don't know much about him. He always had a faraway look you know, the blank eyes, distant stare, all that, kind of creepy if you know what I mean." The owner said.*

*The slaying is the third violent incident in the last several weeks. At each scene, the killer committed suicide with a gun. Despite similarities, the Polizei insist there is no connection.*

*We believe he was a very disturbed young man. His broken childhood coupled with homelessness may have fueled his rage which unfortunately led him to slay Frau Mecklenburg." Hauptmann Tobias Muller said when interviewed.*

Smiling at Muller's cover story Lars folds the paper.

A server rushes to his table with the warm plate.

"Are you finished?" He points to the beer glass.

"Just keep them coming."

"Guten Appetit." the server says with a strange look.

—————— ✦✦✦✦ ——————

## Two A.M.

Lars enters 3995 on the keypad of his Media Markt purchase-a Grundig shortwave radio.

The intro-a baritone voice overlapping a series of recorded thunderclaps, cuts through fuzzy static.

*"**Behold** the Lord cometh with **ten thousands** of his saints, to execute judgment upon all and to convince all that are ungodly of all their ungodly deeds which they have committed and all of their hard speeches which sinners have spoken against him. And now the second golden candlestick, Brother Enoch with a message from Jahweh."*

*"Greetings. I'm brother Enoch and this broadcast is heard nightly on the seventy-five-meter band of your shortwave. I begin a new series called the wages of sin. Roman's six twenty-three says the wages of sin is death..."*

His head bent awkwardly, Lars snores with his mouth hanging open and his arms dangling from his recliner.

# CHAPTER SIXTEEN

"GUTEN MORGEN HERR SCHMIDT."

"Guten Morgen Lars, your hunch was right."

"How so?"

His phone pinched between his shoulder and bent neck Lars unlocks his office.

He tosses his keys on his desk, presses speaker, and starts making coffee.

"All three bodies had the letters jw tattooed in the same spot. Do you know what they mean?" Schmidt asks.

"I have a good idea."

"And you were right to check for Halodan. The lab found slightly high amounts in all three blood samples."

"Could elevated amphetamine levels be a side effect?"

"In some cases, yes, but Halodan is a controlled substance by prescription only."

"I see. Thank you, Doctor Schmidt."

--- ◆◆◆◆◆ ---

*WaldBrunner Gmbh* is one of Germany's rising pharmaceutical companies.

The company website states most of its profits come from experimental drug contracts for everything from cancer to malaria.

Halodan is one of those experimental drugs.

Facing his computer, Lars clicks the description.

*A new antipsychotic drug, Halodan is prescribed for treatment of clinical depression. Dosage is generally one pill taken with meals. Initial symptoms are a warm flushed feeling, tingling in the extremities, increased heart rate, and occasional nausea. These generally take place within fifteen minutes to an hour.*

*Long term side effects are lucid dreams, muscular twitching (in some cases extreme) and feelings of anxiety. Halodan may elevate amphetamine levels. Rare incidents of violent behavior have been recorded.*

Lars rubs his eyes and rereads the last sentence.

*Rare incidents of violent behavior have been recorded.*

"A connection." He says out loud.

His cell phone chimes an incoming text.

*Be in my office at 4 bring everything on the case.*

---

## HAUPTMANN MULLER'S OFFICE: FOUR P.M.

His eyes glued to the pages Hauptmann Muller slowly flips through the case notes.

"Have you checked on Hans Neubauer's friends yet?" he says without looking up.

Lars clears his throat and sits up straight in the visitor's leather chair.

"Yes, he wasn't on his computer much, and those I contacted confirmed his parent's statements. They recalled nothing unusual and even expressed shock."

"What do the numbers on the bodies mean?"

"I'm not sure. They may be a code or an identifier."

"Any theories on the spray-painted x's?"

"All three killers used the same brand–Montana Cans–brick red. And the x may represent the Christian cross."

"Or it's just an X."

"Sir, the murders are too similar to be random. Based on the identical tattoos, the related brutality, and graffiti, I believe we are dealing with a twisted type of serial killing connected with a religious sect called Jahweh's warriors."

"What?"

Muller finally looks up, his eyes narrowing at Lars.

"You said the killers didn't know each other, so how would they be part of a cult?"

"Sir I have a hunch the cult influenced them somehow."

"A cult, here in Frankfurt? Shurtzmann called this morning, the mayor is pressuring him for results. I don't need bizarre hunches."

"A man going by the name Brother Enoch broadcasts on shortwave. I listened to him; his voice matches a sermon on a CD the Neubauer's said their son had."

"Shortwave? That should get him a huge following."

Lars cracks a smile at Muller's rolling eyes.

"There is aa second potential connection. All three killers had traces of an antipsychotic drug named Halodan in their system."

"Now there's a more believable starting point."

"Yes, and I'm troubled by something. Doctor Victor Kolb's signature was on Detlef Bergmeyer's prescription bottle. He also recently recommended it for my brother."

"Check further on that. Meanwhile the *Tagblatt* is still all-over potential names in the Eros Sauna logbook."

"I asked Oom, she thinks an employee might have accidently mentioned it to them." Lars says.

"A logbook that may be evidence, I need it found."

"Evidence for what? A phantom logbook doesn't seem like a priority right now."

"How do we know the killer didn't visit there before?"

"Oom would have told me."

"And that's another thing. If you're screwing her, you need to stop. I need your focus on this case."

His face reddening Lars narrowly glares at Muller.

"Is that all sir?"

"No damn it! The Museumsuferfest is coming up in a few weeks. We are expecting record crowds this year, the last thing we need are stories of a Jim Jones type cult. I need firm answers and I need them fast. Is that understood?"

Looking at the carpet, Lars sighs. "Yes sir."

————————— ✦✦✦✦✦ —————————

## EVENING: KAISERSTRASSE

The *Glockner Apotheke's* last customer of the day, Lars holds up an orange pill bottle and his badge.

"Guten Abend sir I am detective Kubach. What can you tell me about this prescription?"

The bespectacled pharmacist lowers his bifocals, squinting at the label.

"This drug can only be refilled by the patient with doctor verification."

"Verbally or with a written script?"

"A doctor's verbal consent is acceptable. It may be done by phone. Is that why you came here?"

*A quick lie…*

"I'm investigating pill trafficking. Do you know the doctor who prescribed this?"

The pharmacist takes the bottle again.

"I'm sorry sir but I don't recognize that name."

"Can you verify this prescription?"

Bottle in hand, the pharmacist shuffles to the countertop computer.

"That's strange." He says under his breath.

"What is it?"

"Our label is on the bottle but there is no record of this prescription being filled here."

Lars reaches in his shirt pocket.

"It belongs to this young man. Do you recognize him?"

The pharmacist studies Bergmeyer's picture, shaking his head he hands it back.

Lars sighs, he points to a glass display case.

"Let me get some Motrin."

———— ·+·+✦+·+· ————

Lars unclicks his seat belt to reach in his slacks...too late.

He keeps driving, listening to Hauptman Muller's voicemail on speaker.

*"There's been a change of plans. Shurtzmann wants us in his office tomorrow at ten sharp."*

———— ·+·+✦+·+· ————

## SEVEN P.M. LARS KUBACH'S OFFICE

"Guten Abend Herr Neubauer this is detective Lars Kubach."

"Guten Abend sir how may I help you?"

"I'm calling to see if your son was taking any specific medications."

"My apologies Herr Kubach but further questions about our son shall be answered by our attorney."

*No doubt from the Kohler and Schmaltz law firm.*

"Thank you, sir."

He opens his notepad; elbows propped on his desk, his chin resting on his folded hands, he stares intently at the numbers.

16-20, 22-18, 7-27.

He underlines them and scribbles notes.

Dates? Times? A secret code?

*I'm getting nowhere with this.*

Rubbing his tired eyes, he suddenly bolts up straight.

"Wait a minute! Seven two seven. The stork's protest sign matches the number on Mecklenburg's body. There must be a connection!"

---

# Two A.M.

The Museumsuferfest is one of Germany's largest festivals. For three days at the end of August the museums along the River Main stay open late and millions of visitors enjoy live bands, craft booths, and foods from around the world. This year's theme-The Inquisition.

After four Dortmunder Unions, Lars reluctantly agrees with Hauptmann Muller; word of a doomsday cult would be a public relations disaster and bad for business in a city known for business.

Determined to listen to Brother Enoch's entire broadcast he turns on his shortwave.

---

*"Greetings listeners. Tonight, I continue the wages of sin message. I begin on the subjects of swords. Jesus said I come not to send peace but a sword. What did he mean by this?"*

*"The sword represents judgment. John the revelator wrote. 'Repent or I will come quickly and fight against you with the sword of my mouth.'"*

*"Jahweh declared I will bring a sword upon you. The prophet Jeremiah said cursed is he that keeps his sword from blood. Jahweh has given us authority to use the sword so we must use it. Five shall chase a hundred, and a hundred shall put ten thousand to flight, and your enemies shall fall before you by the sword."*

*"Jahweh will judge every work and every secret thing. He has reserved judgement for the wicked and will punish the workers of iniquity with everlasting destruction. The destruction of sinners and transgressors will be by the sword, and they that forsake the Lord shall be consumed."*

"*Violence shall cover the mouth of the wicked. And who will be sorry for them when desolation and famine and sword shall come upon them? Therefore, Jahweh's servants must not hold back the sword, we must prepare for his coming we must reprove the world of its wickedness. For without shedding of blood there is no remission for sins. The righteous shall rejoice and he will wash his feet in the blood of the wicked. And that judgment is according to the truth against them which commit such things. Amen and Amen.*"

# CHAPTER SEVENTEEN

## Thursday Ten A.M. Polizeipräsidium

Lars stands at attention, facing Polizeipräsident Shurtzmann's desk.

Hauptmann Muller watches from the visitor's leather armchair.

After several slurps of coffee Shurtzmann closes the case folder.

"The mayor called me yesterday about your case. She wants a report on her desk tomorrow. Hauptmann Muller..." Shurtzmann glances at him, "says you have a theory?"

"Yes sir, the killings have potential connections to Jahweh's warriors a religious sect led by a man called Brother Enoch."

"I read your notes, please elaborate further."

"Hans Neubauer had a CD sermon narrated by him and Detlef Bergmeyer's shortwave radio was preset to his broadcast. I've listened to him. Mostly he rants and raves about sin."

"Can you prove either of them had any actual contact with this Enoch?"

"I can't confirm that yet, but all three killers had the initials jw tattooed in the same spot under their armpit."

"All of which is circumstantial evidence."

Lars glares at Muller's interruption.

"Hold on." Shurtzmann raises a palm. "Are you suggesting this Enoch character directed them to kill from his radio broadcast?"

"He claims that a faithful remnant of men and women will judge the world before god returns."

"But you have no definitive proof connecting **him** with the killings?" Lars sighs.

"No. However I noticed a protestor's sign matched the numbers on Frau Mecklenburg's body."

"From an unrelated women's rights group?"

Shurtzmann and Muller share doubtful glances.

"Excuse us for a moment. We want to discuss your theory privately. Please step outside."

Ten minutes later Shurtzmann hands Lars the case folder.

"We went over the merits of your report. You noted the killers had trace amounts of a drug for depression but whether it drove them to kill is debatable. The religious angle might have some basis, but you need more evidence before we can consider it."

"Excuse me sir but this sect is borderline dangerous."

"Not according to the *sect watch* article in your file. For now, we will continue to attribute Frau Mecklenburg's murder to an angry young adult with a troubled past."

"Just like the other two, a good stall tactic." Lars says dryly, ignoring Muller's reddening face.

Shurtzmann stands up, hands on his hips he paces behind his desk.

He turns sharply, his hard-squint locks on Lars.

"So far, I see nothing but speculation from you! It's bad enough we have a heat wave and an African gang, robbing tourists. Mayor Hagen doesn't want our city labeled unsafe to visit. Since I am now forced to stall, I suggest you come up with definitive results! Do you understand?"

"Yes sir."

"You are dismissed."

———— ‹•••••› ————

## Oɴᴇ P.M. Bᴀʜɴʜᴏғsᴠɪᴇʀᴛᴇʟ Pᴏʟɪᴢᴇɪ Sᴛᴀᴛɪᴏɴ

"Wilhelm Kugel was caught smoking opium with a runaway teenage girl."

On a video chat with attorney Mira Klosterman Lars scrolls through the sect watch article on his computer.

"How was he charged with pimping?"

"She said he forced her to prostitute to support their habits. He admitted only to *encouraging* her. Of course, we knew it was bullshit. What is your interest in the incident Herr Kubach?"

"He may be involved in a case I'm on. I need information on him, an old address perhaps?"

"That doesn't surprise me. He always was a smooth talker. I'll check his probation records and send you what I find."

---

## Fᴏᴜʀ P.M.

His feet propped on his desk Lars stops reading Kicker Sportmagazin's weekly Bundesliga predictions to answer his ringing cell phone.

"Guten tag Lars." A faintly familiar voice says.

"Hey... Andreas Loewe! Guten tag to you as well. It's been a while. What's new?"

"I called to tell you my band is in Frankfurt this weekend."

"You have a band?"

"Yes, after leaving the Polizei I became a drummer for *Die Gefroren Geister.*"

"The *Frozen Ghosts*-interesting name. What genre?"

"Gothic rock, our first CD comes out next month."

"Good for you, I'm a Volks Festival fan myself."

"We'll be at *Angelica's* in Sachsenhausen at ten Saturday you're welcome to come."

"I'll see you there, talk to you then."

His phone chimes an incoming text.

*Hi Lars, sent you an email with Herr Kugel's last known address. Hope it helps.*

<hr>

## EVENING: FRANKFURT WESTEND

Parked under a hedge maple's leafy shade, Lars watches a strawberry blonde in sandals and tight Capris walking a honey-brown Pomeranian.

On her second pass he lowers his power window and subtly displays his badge.

"Excuse me I'm detective Lars Kubach. Do you live next to that apartment?"

She follows his eyes to a three-story khaki-painted building partially hidden by a vine covered iron fence.

"Yes…" she says hesitantly.

The yapping Pomeranian tugs at its leash.

"Hush, baby," she stoops and gives the leash two slight tugs.

The dog sits and licks her hand gazing up at her and wagging its tail.

"You have him well trained."

"Thank you, his name is Oliver. And I'm Giselle Rosenblatt."

"I'm sorry to bother you Frau Rosenblatt but what can you tell me about the neighbors?"

Her eyes shift back to the building.

"Let's get off the street. I'll make us some iced tea."

<hr>

Lars turns away fending off Oliver's frenzied attempts to lick his face.

"Oliver, stop and go lay down!" Giselle commands from her kitchenette.

Oliver leaps off the sofa. Nails clicking loudly, he scampers across the wood floor to a pet bed in the corner.

Resting his head on his paws his eyes dart back and forth.

"Nice apartment." Lars says scanning a wall of framed animal pictures. "Lots of exotic animals."

"Thank you I'm a veterinarian at the Frankfurt Zoo."

Her sandals flapping, she crosses the living room carrying two steaming ceramic mugs.

"I made honey lemon."

"Thank you."

She sets them on coasters on a coffee table and sits in a high-backed vinyl chair across from Lars.

"They moved in about a year ago just a few people at first, now about twenty."

"Any odd behavior?"

"They dress old fashioned and don't come out much. They're quiet except for Friday nights and Saturday mornings."

"What do they do?"

"I believe they have a church service, sometimes I hear music and singing."

"Do they have visitors?"

"Occasionally on Friday nights."

"Is that their white van parked out front?"

"I think so, it's there often."

"Have you seen a women's group entering or leaving?"

Giselle shakes her head.

"They did have some renovations a while back."

"Renovations?"

"Yes, an interior design company did the work."

Lars unzips his notebook and hands her three pictures.

"Have you seen these men enter or leave at any time?"

Shaking her head, Giselle hands them back.

"Sorry sir but I have not."

She brushes a hair strand from her face.

*Her blonde hair...sparkling blue eyes...athletic build...a younger Inga...*

"Are you ok?"

Lars blinks several times and rubs his eyes.

"Yes, I'm just a little tired."

He finishes his tea gently setting the mug down.

"I didn't mean to interrogate you Frau Rosenblatt, it's part of an investigation. Thank you for your time and hospitality."

"Sure anytime." She says with an infectious smile.

---

The white van is a newer model Mercedes Benz Sprinter.

Lars copies the license number in his notebook.

He squeezes the Saab from his parking spot and drives slowly past a row of tightly parked cars.

A flash in his rearview mirror makes him look back at the apartment.

The fading sun's last rays reflect from the tip of an antenna mast poking above the roof.

# CHAPTER EIGHTEEN

### FRIDAY AFTERNOON: BAHNHOFSVIERTEL STATION

"SIR, CAN I SPEAK WITH YOU?"

"Come in Lars."

Lars closes Hauptmann Muller's door.

"I may have found the sect address."

"You may have?"

"It's brother Enoch's last known address. I searched the land register records; the buyer was a woman named Mariana Obermayer."

"Is she a member of the sect?"

"I'm not sure yet, but here's where it gets interesting. According to the selling agent the previous owner failed to make tax and mortgage payments. Frau Obermayer paid the taxes and bought it cash–two hundred thousand Euros."

Muller raises his eyebrows.

"That's rare, how did that avoid scrutiny?"

"The agent didn't demand financial disclosure, he was happy to sell, it was on the market close to six months."

"Curious but not unusual."

"There's more, a neighbor claims the building holds religious services and I spotted an antenna mast behind the roof. I think Enoch is using the building for a church and may be broadcasting from there. *Bauer*

*Hausdesigners* did some interior renovations right after its purchase. Someone had to pay for that too."

"So far nothing is illegal based on your observations. However, something needs to happen quick. The mayor chewed our asses out this morning, she's not quite ready for the cult angle without better evidence."

"So, what is our next step?"

"Concentrate on the group members, find out more."

———— ✦✦✦✦✦ ————

**FRIDAY EVENING: WESTEND**

Dressed casually in khaki slacks and a tan, short sleeve Jack Wolfskin Polo, Lars straightens his matching flat cap and adjusts his fake wire rimmed glasses.

A Bible tucked under his arm he follows a cobblestone path to the building, stopping to read a bilingual sign posted on the door.

*ALLES WILKOMMEN / ALL WELCOME*

Hearing singing inside he presses the doorbell.

A shuffling smiling usher directs him to a bench along the back wall of a studio apartment type room.

Frau Rosenblatt was right-the women wear ankle length dark dresses, the men–slacks and dress shirts.

Some stand and clap. A young man in the front row sways with his eyes closed and arms spread skyward.

Pretending to flip through a hymnal book Lars sneaks a glance at a familiar tall woman tapping a tambourine on her wrist.

*"So...the **stork** is a member?"*

He scans the other women's faces, matching them to the Eros Sauna protest.

The blonde buzz cut keyboardist abruptly stops playing, and everyone takes a seat.

Wearing a flowing lavender robe, Brother Enoch strides to the pulpit with a book tucked under one arm.

He sets it down and raises his arms.

His eyes shift immediately to Lars, he takes an exaggerated deep breath.

"In the last days, men shall be lovers of themselves, covetous, boasters, proud, blasphemers, disobedient to parents, unthankful, unholy. Traitors, heady, high minded, and lovers of pleasures more than lovers of God."

Another deep breath.

"They have a form of godliness, but they deny the power always learning but never knowing the truth. We must turn from them for they will proceed no further. Their sins and folly will be manifest before all."

"These reprobates withstand the truth just as Jannes and Jambres withstood Moses. Jahweh declares that we wrestle not against flesh and blood but against principalities and powers against rulers of darkness and spiritual wickedness in high places."

Scattered claps and amen shouts rise from the congregation. The keyboardist raises his hands in worship.

"We see television scandals of the rich and famous! Our politicians and rulers are corrupted by bribes! The bankers worship mammon and sell their souls for power! But their fate was prophesied when the angels showed Enoch a vision of destruction. I read now from the book of Enoch."

He thumbs through the book on the pulpit.

"*And into heaven they shall not ascend. And on the earth, they shall not come. Such shall be the lot of sinners who deny the name of the Lord of spirits, and are preserved for the day of suffering and tribulation.*"

Brother Enoch looks up, his eyes flicker to Lars.

"Jahweh warned Noah that he had condemned the world and ordered him to build the ark."

Brother Enoch turns a page.

"I return to the words of the first Enoch."

"*And after that my grandfather Enoch took hold of me and raised me up and said to me, Go for I have asked the Lord of spirits as touching this commotion on the earth. And he said to me, Because of their unrighteousness their judgment has been determined and shall not be withheld by me. Because of the sorceries which they have searched out and learned, the earth and those who dwell upon it shall be destroyed. And they have no place of repentance forever, because they have shown them what was hidden, and they are the damned but as for thee, my son, the Lord of Spirits knows that thou art pure, and guiltless of this reproach concerning the secrets."*

Brother Enoch closes the book.

"The first Enoch was shown a mystery. And now I the second Enoch have seen the same. Jahweh has raised **me** to condemn the world and lead a remnant into the safety of the ark. Let us conclude with prayer and songs. Our father who art in heaven..."

———— ✦✦✦✦✦ ————

Flanked by the keyboardist Enoch flashes a forced smile and extends his bony blue veined wrist.

Lars accepts his clammy handshake.

"Did you enjoy our service?"

"Very interesting."

"We are doing God's work. Our mission is to warn the world to repent before Jahweh's glorious appearing."

Lars nods again.

"And how sir is your spiritual life?"

"I'm Catholic, I've done the sacraments."

"That's fine but where do you stand with Jahweh?"

"I probably should go to confession." Lars chuckles.

"Well, if you need to talk about matters of faith, we are here for you. Feel free to contact us anytime."

"I will, thank you sir."

They share a second handshake.

*"What a kook."* Lars says quietly on his way out.

# CHAPTER NINETEEN

## SACHSENHAUSEN: SATURDAY EVENING

HOLDING HANDS LARS AND OOM stroll down Alt Sachsenhausen's narrow cobblestone side streets.

They pass rows of loud, packed bars, weaving through rowdy crowds waiting to enter thumping clubs.

"There it is!"

Oom points to a black strobe light above *Angelica's*.

A wood carved golem statue guards the entrance.

A ticket checker in a black top hat lets them in.

His ears ringing from pounding bass, Lars surveys the inside–tables circling a compact dance floor, blacklight tubes framing the ceiling, and a raised stage for the band.

The first floor is for dancing and live bands. Roped off stairs lead to a private lower floor-nicknamed *Die Kink Raum*.

There are the usual rumors–it's a BDSM dungeon, an upscale fetish club, a drug den.

Or, as the club's owner claims… 'a place to unwind.'

Only those who pay the high member fee really know.

"Let's get drinks." Oom shouts.

Sidestepping a waitress in a low-cut black leather corset and knee-high boots balancing a drink tray, Oom pulls him by the arm to the bar counter.

They squeeze into two barstools between goth girls with black fingernails, eyeliner, and coiffed black hair, and a man dressed as Nosferatu–complete with fake vampire teeth and ghoulish white makeup.

Lars instantly feels out of place in his leather jacket, faded Die Toten Hosen T shirt, and jeans tucked into old Bundeswehr boots.

Oom's black vinyl mini skirt, stiletto ankle boots, and torn black fishnet stockings blend right in.

Lars warily eyes a stuffed raven perched over the bar.

A pierced lipped bartender with a black mesh shirt, silver skull earrings, and a pentagram necklace sets down two coasters and stands silent like the golem outside.

"Ein Maisel's Weisse." Lars shouts over She's Dangerous by Clan of Xymox.

Oom playfully slaps his arm.

"Get a blue blood instead. You will like."

She winks at the stone-faced bartender and holds up two fingers.

Cupping his hand Lars leans close to Oom's ear.

"I thought this style went out in the nineties."

"It never goes away. What you know about the band?"

"Their drummer worked a few cases with me."

Lars waves at Andreas arranging his drums on the stage.

Wearing leather chaps and a silver studded black jacket, his neat Polizei haircut is a memory, replaced by snaky blond dreadlocks.

He waves back and gives Lars a thumbs up.

"The Polizei let him look like that?"

Lars laughs at Oom's surprised face.

"No but if he could, he would have. He always was a free spirit."

The bartender sets down a wooden test tube rack holding two test tubes of glowing blue liquor.

Eyeing them skeptically, Lars takes one.

"Drink." Oom shouts.

Lars follows her lead, tilting and draining it in one swallow.

He coughs and shakes his head vigorously.

Oom flashes her toothy grin.

"You like it?"

"Tastes different than it looks…like hot peppermint."

Holding up the empty tubes Oom waves at the bartender.

"Two more." She shouts.

Lars reaches across the bar counter, picking up a *Die Gefroren Geister* flyer from a stack.

His head pounding, he reads the scheduled song list.

*Father Nimrod*

*Cold day in Hades*

*The Nephilim Return*

Two thumping concert speakers abruptly stop.

Amid scattered cheers, the lights slowly dim.

The emaciated lead singer slings a two-necked electric guitar over his shoulder.

He snatches a microphone and flashes a victory sign.

"Are you ready?" he screams hoarsely.

A deafening roar fills the bar.

"Bloody awesome!"

He opens a coffin shaped suitcase, handing out ghost faced masks to the three band members.

He slips his on and twirls a finger over his head.

Two LED color blocks instantly flood the stage with blinding red, white, and green lights.

A fog machine spits out curling jets of white smoke.

Crisscrossing red and green laser lights pierce the haze settling over the dance floor.

Oom turns Lars to her, thrusting a test tube in his face.

"Open wide."

He tilts back, she empties the shot down his throat.

His last memories…the lead singer's screaming lyrics, and Oom's warm lips meeting his.

## Sunday: The Der Frankfurter Hotel

Shivering in spasms, Lars peels back a clinging sweaty bedsheet, yawns, and massages his pounding temples.

Sitting up bare-chested he stretches his stiff back and stares at the faded *Angelica's* ink stamp still on his wrist.

Last night returns in fragments-*catching up with Andreas over liter mugs of Weisen...warm apple wine shots at Doris Winehaus...staggering with Oom down the cobblestone side streets...her erratic driving while he nods off...and*-he smiles-*intense sweaty sex in a king-sized bed.*

Still shivering he shuts off the blasting icy air conditioner.

Oom is gone.

He picks up his phone from the nightstand, the screen reads one P.M. and he has a text.

*Don't fall in love with me.*

---

"You left?"

"Yes, I am at Sauna now. We reopen Monday. I leave car for you at hotel."

"Why the text?"

"You not remember? You sex with me, say I love you many times, ask me to marry. I think you miss your ex-wife."

"I did all that?"

He cringes at Oom's familiar high-pitched laugh.

"No problem. You need to release male energy. I call you later."

---

## Four P.M. The Kaiser Bistro

Intently watching Sky Deutschland's Bundesliga highlights, Lars sips a glass of fizzing Spezi.

His hangover is gone thanks to a hot shower, a round of boxing combinations, and a riverfront jog.

Expecting Oom he immediately grabs his vibrating phone off the bar counter.

"Herr Kubach this is Doctor Grunheim from the *Saint Timothy Krankenhaus.*"

"What is it?" Lars says guardedly.

Doctor Grunheim releases a drawn-out sigh.

"You need to come here right away."

Hands trembling Lars drains the glass and slams it on the counter rattling the ice cubes.

———————————

A white-haired security guard behind a u-shaped desk, squints at Lars and his badge.

"Wait in the lobby." He orders curtly.

Ten agonizing minutes later a solemn Doctor Grunheim enters the lobby.

"Where is he?" Lars asks his eyes growing wide.

"We found him slumped in his wheelchair. He wasn't breathing and had no pulse. A staff member tried to revive him. We rushed him to emergency but-"

"No! No! Oh no!"

Lars pushes past Doctor Grunheim's outstretched arms and races to the elevator.

# CHAPTER TWENTY

## WEDNESDAY: SAINT ELIZABETH CHURCH

THE FUNERAL SERVICE OVER, LARS kneels next to Peter's casket. In the now silent church, he closes his eyes.

*A grim-faced Doctor Hassan Gummadi enters the Koblenz Bundeswehr Medical Center waiting room.*

*Lars and his mother rise expectantly from white plastic chairs.*

*"How is he?" Erika Kubach asks, her face ashen.*

*"He is still critical."*

*"How critical?" Lars asks.*

*The swarthy surgeon reads from his clipboard.*

*"He has brain trauma, a broken collarbone, and a shattered pelvis. I am sorry for being so straightforward, but we couldn't save his left leg."*

*Erika's trembling hands cover her mouth.*

*"Oh, dear God my poor baby."*

*Lars wraps his arm around her. Shuddering with sobs she buries her face in his shoulder.*

*Lars and doctor Gummadi share helpless frowns.*

*Doctor Gummadi tenderly pats Erika's shoulder.*

*"He made it this far. We will do everything for him."*

*"Thank you doctor Gummadi." Lars says.*

*Erika dabs her teary face with a handkerchief.*

*"Can we see him?"*

*"It may not be a good time."*

*"I don't care."*

*Side by side Lars and his mother silently stare at the maze of tubes and blinking humming machines hooked up to Peter's broken body.*

*"He looks peaceful." Erika whispers.*

---

*"He looks peaceful…"*

Lars staggers from Peter's casket on rubbery legs.

He flinches when Father Grienke, the priest presiding over the funeral Mass grips his shoulder.

"You need a private place to grieve come with me."

The grey bearded priest guides Lars to his office.

"Take all the time you need, and don't be afraid to call upon the Lord."

---

**WEDNESDAY EVENING**

At her apartment window, retired nurse Frau Mildred Geiger sips tea watching pouring rain from a thunderstorm-and a man walking unsteadily to the building.

Her intercom buzzes.

*"A bit late for a visitor."*

She shuffles to her door and presses talk.

"Hello who is it?"

"Lars Kubach."

"Lars? What brings you here?"

"I'm sorry to arrive unannounced but I need to talk."

---

His head down, Lars sways in the hallway.

"Look at you you're soaking wet."

"It's still raining. I apologize." He slurs.

"And a good bit drunk as well. You didn't drive?"

Lars shakes his head.

"I took the Strassenbahn."

"Come in and dry off. I have more tea steeping in the kitchen."

His trembling hands wrapped around a steaming ceramic mug Lars takes a grateful sip.

"Lars, I'm not used to seeing you like this, what's wrong?"

He turns to hide the tears welling in his eyes.

"I buried my brother today."

"Oh, dear I am so sorry for you."

"He killed himself, the doctors' suspect an overdose."

Frau Geiger leans across the kitchen table, tenderly pressing her palm on his hand.

"We go back a long way you can talk with me."

A weak smile crosses his tear-streaked face.

"My mother was a devout Catholic. My brother was an atheist. In the last eight months I lost them both. I wanted to confess to the priest after the funeral, but I couldn't do it. I don't know what to believe any more."

"That's common in such a crisis."

"I feel responsible for Peter's death. He reached out to me but all I saw was his anger and not his pain."

"Your brother knows you cared, and at least now he is in a better place. You must continue to move forward difficult as it is."

"That's the problem, when he needed me, I was too much in a hurry to go to work. I ignored him, and I suppressed my mother's death. I wonder if what I do is worth it."

"Don't blame yourself Lars, what you do helps people."

"It doesn't help me! I'm so absorbed by my job I neglect those closest to me. It cost me my marriage, my brother and maybe even part of myself!"

"You need to reset. A vacation maybe."

"I am off for a few days."

"No Lars, a real time away. I was a nurse for thirty years I know all about long hours and dedication. Some time off is a difference maker."

His left hand cupped over his mouth he stares at a Catholic portrait of Jesus on the kitchen wall behind her.

"What keeps you so strong in the faith?"

"When you've seen as much as I have there are things that make sense only if they came from God. Remember the good things about your loved ones and let the rest go, it will take time, but you will pull through."

"I'm not so sure."

"Of course, you are. I see what's wrong with you."

"What is it?"

"You have never allowed yourself to grieve for all your losses. You admit to letting work fill the void."

Propping his elbows on the table, Lars folds his hands under his chin, focusing on the portrait.

Frau Geiger gently pats his shoulder.

"Don't fight it." She whispers.

His lip quivers, he shudders and buries his head in his arms-heaving and sobbing silently on the table.

---

## SUNDAY EVENING

Finished shaving four days of facial hair Lars splashes on aftershave.

He pauses in Oom's bathroom door staring at her.

Eyes closed; she stands tiptoed in the living room with one knee raised-her outstretched fingers curled like claws in front of her face.

Her open robe exposes her smooth caramel stomach and newest tattoo-paw tracks running up her inner thighs.

"What are you doing?" he asks.

"It called pouncing tiger."

"How appropriate."

After a set of slow rhythmic twists, her eyes pop open; she smiles at him.

"Do you want to go out?"

"No, I return to work tomorrow. I need to relax. What you're doing seems like a good way, what is it called?"

"Tai chi, come I show you."

"I'm drunk but I guess I'll try it."

For the next hour Oom laughs at Lars stumbling and swaying through the high horse, crane, and cat stances.

The lesson ends with her on the sofa massaging his lower back with her bare feet.

"You have lot of tension."

"Tell me about Buddhism."

"It is awakening. There are four noble truths-Dukkha, Samudaya, Nirhodha, and Magga."

"What do they mean?"

"I give you simple answer. Number one truth-life is suffering but all things have an end."

"That's it?"

"No, you must know yourself."

He laughs nervously.

"Ok I am Lars Kubach, and I am suffering right now."

"Number two truth, unhappiness with material things causes suffering."

"We suffer because we are not satisfied? How do we stop that?"

"By number three truth, to stop suffering, practice not wanting worldly things. This helps number one truth."

"We can train to stop being materialistic?"

"Yes, meditate every day and follow the eight-fold path. Maybe I give you book you read and learn more."

Hearing a snort, she looks down.

His face pressed sideways in the carpet Lars snores like a purring cat.

# CHAPTER TWENTY-ONE

## MONDAY MORNING: BAHNHOFSVIERTEL POLIZEI STATION

*Y*OUR BROTHER'S TOXICOLOGY REPORT IS *in. Really think you should see it.*
Reading Medical Examiner Schmidt's just arrived email, Lars doesn't hear the approaching footsteps.

Hauptmann Muller's knock startles him.

"Guten Morgen Lars welcome back. Are you ok?"

"Yes sir, I'm taking it one day at a time."

"That's good it's all you can do. Anyway, the reason I'm here is this."

He hands Lars two tickets.

Lars smiles broadly.

"Touchline seats? Thank you, sir."

"At home against Bayern München. I know you like the Bundesliga, so I used a connection to get them. Take Oom with you, but please… don't get another knot this time."

Lars laughs at Muller's exaggerated rolling eyes.

"I won't sir."

"That's the good news now the bad. During your week off priority was given to the African gang. They did two robberies in one night. The mayor wants your case updated by the end of the week. See what you can do to connect the dots."

---

## AFTERNOON: FRANKFURT MORGUE

Medical examiner Schmidt leans over his desk offering a sympathetic handshake.

"Herr Kubach, I'm sorry about your brother."

"Thank you."

"We checked for Halodan as you requested."

Schmidt waits silently as Lars reads the results.

"According to this Peter had a lethal amount in his system. So, he did overdose?"

Schmidt nods solemnly.

"This drug has dangerous side effects and raises amphetamine levels which may cause violent behavior." Lars says.

"You did your homework. During clinical trials, some subjects became violent after taking it. But I must stress that this occurred only with high dosages."

"Yet it was still approved?"

Tight lipped, Schmidt shrugs.

"Explain what would happen in an overdose?"

"Extreme amounts would likely result in massive heart failure."

Head down, Lars sighs and covers his forehead with his right palm; he looks up biting his lip.

"Thank you, Herr Schmidt. You have been helpful, now I have something to go on."

--------------------

## EVENING: SAINT TIMOTHY KRANKENHAUS MENTAL WARD

"My apologies for calling you in early Doctor Kolb, but according to Peter's death report he overdosed on Halodan, the drug you prescribed."

Finished buttoning his hospital jacket, Doctor Kolb looks at Lars with his hands in his pockets.

"Yes, it seems he saved the pills instead of taking them."

"And no one thought to make sure he took them and prevent such a thing?"

His face suddenly flushing, Kolb's eyes narrow defensively.

"I only prescribe medicines. An orderly administers the dosages."

"You prescribed it for his outbursts. Yet one of its side effects is violent behavior. Correct me if I am wrong but that sounds like a contradictory treatment method."

"Only in extremely rare cases. Halodan is for patients diagnosed as clinically depressed. It is safe if properly administered."

"So, failure to discover my brother hid enough to overdose would not be considered properly administered now, would it?"

Kolb releases an exasperated sigh.

"These young men come here with prior issues. I am not responsible for a patient's behavior." He snaps.

"Yet you prescribe them an experimental behavior altering drug."

"Your brother was depressed sir."

Lars glares hotly at Kolb's defiant face.

"You also treated Matthias Hinkel and Detlef Bergmeyer. Both commit violent crimes, and my brother commits suicide. I think this drug is dangerous."

Kolb crosses his arms.

"You need to take that up with the manufacturer, excuse me detective, but I have nothing else to say."

# CHAPTER TWENTY-TWO

## TUESDAY: LARS KUBACH'S OFFICE

HIS NOTEBOOK OPEN ON HIS desk Lars types FDZ 11 in the Polizei's automobile database.

"A two thousand ten Mercedes Benz registered to Nigel Trotter-a non-German name interesting, let's look him up."

Five minutes later Nigel Trotter's driver license is on his screen.

"A class B German license, issued in Frankfurt earlier this year."

* * *

Logged into *biosketch.com*. Lars summarizes Nigel Trotter's basic background profile out loud.

"Birthplace, Cardiff England, fifty-nine years old. Education, a bachelor's degree in human behavior from Cardiff school for Humanities and a master's degree in clinical psychology from London University. Speaks fluent German. Currently employed at *Klaus Moritz Übergangszentrum* Frankfurt Germany. Previous address *Seven Highbury Street* London, England."

Lars brings up the German license database again.

"Interesting, if he's a foreigner he should have had an EU license previously, but I don't see any record. Something doesn't add up."

* * *

## Afternoon: Near Frankfurt Osthafen (East Harbor)

A center for troubled youth, the *Klaus Moritz Übergangszentrum*'s office overlooks a shuttered warehouse with a weed choked vacant lot.

Waiting for an answer to his knock, Lars surveys the Osthafen's huge looming dock crane and long rows of double stacked metal cargo containers in the distance.

Nearby, under the watchful eye of a man with a whistle, two teams of young boys play soccer in an uneven field with traffic cones for goals.

A wide shot on goal lands at his feet, he smiles and returns it with a curling sweep kick.

The boys stop to stare at him shaking hands with a woman in her mid-forties with sunken cheeks and tired eyes.

"Guten tag Herr Kubach. I'm Frau Attiger. You wish to ask me some questions?"

"Yes, if you don't mind."

"Here here! Now stop that! Excuse me detective."

Frau Attiger rushes past him to break up two boys wrestling in a tangled heap.

Dodging wild swings and kicks she helps the youth sport coach separate them.

Lars smiles watching her stand over them wagging a finger.

Side by side with their heads down they exchange hugs and race back to the field.

---

"I'm sorry Herr Kubach but these kids can be a handful at times." she says between winded breaths.

"The skinny one had a mean left hook I could make him a good boxer."

Frau Attiger copies his smile.

"We get them from all over, runaways, trafficked girls, abused boys. We're struggling for funding to move out of this old distribution center. Come inside."

---

A long-necked oscillating fan barely stirs the sweltering humid air in Frau Attiger's office.

Seated across from her obvious surplus office desk, Lars slyly scans the peeling plaster, water-stained drop ceiling, and threadbare curtains.

He takes out his pocket notebook and clicks a pen.

"You may refuse to answer any questions, but I would appreciate your cooperation."

"No problem, sir."

"Do you have an employee named Nigel Trotter?"

"Yes, he mentors the more troubled youth. Nice dresser, kind of quiet, has a child psychology degree."

Lars looks up from writing.

"How long has he worked here?"

"We hired him in January this year."

"Does he have an office?"

"Yes, but its locked. He works Monday Wednesday and Friday."

"He listed this address as his residence. Does he stay here?"

"No sir this is strictly a transitional shelter until we find homes for the youth, our rooms are only for them and volunteer staff members."

"This may sound unusual but is he a religious person?"

Frau Attiger thoughtfully purses her lips.

"I believe so. I've seen a bible on his desk."

"One last question, I'm doing an investigation, do you recognize any of these young men?"

Frau Attiger studies the pictures Lars hands her.

"I remember this one, quiet and shy."

"Do you remember his name?"

"I think it was Detlef, but I'm not sure. He was too old to stay here but Nigel let him volunteer in his office. We would feed him in exchange for that and some small labor tasks."

"Did mister Trotter counsel him?"

"I don't think so."

Closing his notebook, Lars clears his throat sounding official.

"Frau Attiger, this is part of an investigation. For security reasons I must insist you not mention a word of this to anyone including mister Trotter."

---

## EVENING: THE KAISER BISTRO

Ruggedly handsome with a swimmer's build and ice blue eyes, Manfred Schollner scans the Kaiser Bistro's sparse late evening crowd.

He spots Lars discreetly waving from a corner booth.

They shake hands and Lars offers him a seat.

"Good to see you, old friend."

"Likewise, Herr Schollner."

"So, this is your new hangout? I remember it used to be *Gotz's Bierstube.*"

"Yeah, but I've come to like this place better."

"You look a little haggard."

"It's true I'm working a tough case and dealing with my brother's suicide."

"Peter? Oh my God. I'm sorry to hear that. Are you ok?"

"I will be, things are coming from all directions."

A hostess with close-cropped blonde hair sets two tall glasses of foamy Hefe Weisen on coasters.

"What would you like to eat?" she asks.

"A Brötchen with ham and cheese." Lars says.

"And the same for me."

She blushes at Schollner's flirting wink.

Lars takes a long swallow; he glances around and lowers his voice. "Have you heard of the recent murders here?"

Schollner nods with his hands folded under his chin.

"It's making news beyond Hessen."

"I suspect a religious sect, but each killer also had traces of Halodan, a prescription drug for depression, the same drug my brother overdosed on."

"And you think there is a connection to the killings?"

"Yes, in fact I believe it may be responsible."

"What evidence do you have for this?"

"Peter's doctor prescribed it for one of the killers and a second killer was one of his patients. It seems more than coincidental."

"What's the doctor's name?"

"Victor Kolb. He works at the *Saint Timothy Krankenhaus*."

"Do you suspect his involvement?"

"I'm not sure yet, but he seemed defensive when we talked."

"Your hunches are usually right. The drug theory seems valid."

"Indeed, but my chief is skeptical, especially of the possible sect involvement. Since you still work for Interpol's Wiesbaden center, I could use your help with info on Doctor Kolb."

---

An hour later, Lars sets down his fourth empty glass.

"We sure had some good times together, the Bundeswehr, the academy, and the Polizei. Busting Turks and Africans in the eighties and Russian gangs after the wall fell."

Schollner nods and downs a handful of peanuts, he leans back, his smiling face nostalgic.

"The undercover surveillance was fun, the drunk leaning against a pillar, the bum asking for change."

"Yeah, shadowing suspects in an Imbiss line or pretending to wait at a streetcar stop. You never know maybe I'll work with you after I retire."

Still grinning, Schollner empties his Weisen.

"Are you ok?"

Lars snaps awake, he rubs his bloodshot eyes.

"Sorry I drifted off there. I'll pay for the beers."

He drunkenly pulls two twenty Euro notes from his pants pocket, sliding them under his coaster.

He grips Schollner's hand tightly.

"It was good to see you, old friend."

"You too Lars, I'll be in Frankfurt for a few days. I'll get that info on Doctor Kolb. Do you need a ride home?"

"I'm good. Oom will pick me up."

"Oom?" Schollner arches an eyebrow.

"My semi girlfriend."

He winks and staggers to the exit jabbing his phone keypad.

# CHAPTER TWENTY-THREE

**H**IS OFFICE DOOR LOCKED; LARS raises the volume on *Cults in our Midst* a two-part You Tube video narrated by German cult expert Pastor Lucas Gottleib.

*"In his sermon on the mount Jesus warned of a time when false apostles and false Christ's would come. Let no man deceive you he said, for many will come in my name saying I am Christ and will deceive many. Well listeners that time is now with the rise of false doctrines and cults. A cult is a religious group that denies or changes all or some of the basic Christian tenants or fundamentals. Most share an apocalyptic end-times view in which only they will survive. Often, they are founded or led by a charismatic self-appointed leader or messiah. The leader controls followers by exploiting individual weaknesses. Generally, **his** word and theology are accepted as truth or law. Members often display zealous and unquestioning support for the leader and his doctrines whether he is alive or dead."*

*"A person dealing with a failed relationship, a family tragedy, job loss, depression, guilt, stress, or other personal issues is easily persuaded to accept the leader as an authority figure."*

*"Members stay even if they have reservations because they are led to believe that God has given the leader a divine revelation or mission and ordained him as an earthly representative. The leader dictates the member's actions, thoughts, and feelings sometimes to extremes such as forbidding*

*marriage or relationships, controlling work, diet, and manner of dress and appearance. Members are often pressured to renounce family and friends for the greater good of the cult. Fear, guilt, and intimidation are used to discourage privacy and independent thought. Anyone considering leaving is told that their departure will remove them from God's will. In part two we will examine..."*

Lars exits the video, rubs his eyes, and leans back in his chair.

Moments later he is fast asleep.

---

## AFTERNOON: *PINK PLATZ*, FRANKFURT'S GAY SECTION

"That's the second time this week! I'm installing a camera immediately. We'll catch the little bastards."

Hands on his hips, Teddy Van Halst, the owner of *Club Bacchus*, glares at the red spray-painted words *God is not mocked* on the bar's front door.

His bouncer-a fake tanned chiseled muscular giant points to a line of silent women carrying signs.

"What about them?"

"They're just a bunch of dried-up breeders, jealous that men don't want them anymore."

Van Halst snorts and flips his middle finger.

The women lower their signs and file into a waiting white van.

"They left this behind."

The bouncer hands Van Halst a booklet.

"Sin and the human condition, ha what do they know?"

Smirking, Van Halst deliberately shreds the tract as the van passes. He turns to the bouncer.

"See what you can do about removing that graffiti. And here, throw this shit out too."

He drops the pieces into the bouncer's cupped palm.

---

# Evening

Still sweating from his jog, Lars locks his apartment mailbox.
Halfway up the first flight of stairs his phone rings.
He puts Manfred Schollner on speaker.
"Guten Abend Lars, you may be on to something."
"What did you find?"
"Doctor Victor Kolb has worked at the Frankfurt clinic since two thousand eight."
"I know that."
Lars trudges up the second flight.
"Well, here's something I bet you didn't know. His resume shows a degree in psychopathology, but a *Mainz University* records clerk found no graduation records for anyone named Victor Kolb."
"Are you suggesting his credentials might be fake?"
"Yes. He also worked at the *Mannheim Mental Health Klinik* before that."
Lars sighs, *last flight...*
"Thank you, my friend. It looks like a busy day tomorrow. Email what you have to my home computer."

# CHAPTER TWENTY-FOUR

**THURSDAY MORNING: FRANKFURT HAUPTBAHNHOF**

STANDING UNDER A GIANT BANNER ad for Tchibo Coffee, Lars hurriedly chews a warm bratwurst sandwich.

He checks the clock above track seven. The Mannheim ICE departs in five minutes.

Wiping a crumb from his lip, he rushes to the long, crowded platform, darting past travelers dragging wheeled suitcases.

+ + + + + +

"Die Karte bitte."

Eyes half closed, Lars hands his ticket to a porter in a blue blazer and peaked cap with the familiar red DB logo.

He hands the punched ticket back with an obligatory smile.

Lars glances out the speeding train's windows at Frankfurt's fading skyline behind them.

Expected arrival time in Mannheim-thirty-five minutes.

He yawns, shifts in his seat, and resumes his nap.

*"Mannheim Mental Health clinic how may I help you?"* A woman's *voice says.*

*"Detective Lars Kubach Frankfurt Polizei. I am inquiring about a doctor who used to work there."*

*"The name Bitte."*

*"Doctor Victor Kolb."*

*On hold, Lars takes a long sip of Jacob's Coffee.*

*"Sir?"*

*"Yes."*

*"Doctor Kolb worked in the psychosomatic Medicine and psychotherapy department."*

*"Do you have the names of any patients under his care?"*

*"I cannot disclose that over the phone sir. I can refer you to our head doctor."*

*"Thank you."*

*On hold again, he tunes his office radio to the morning traffic report. Autobahn Five near the Frankfurter Kreuz is bumper to bumper due to ongoing construction.*

*"It'll be quicker by train." He sighs.*

———— ·✦✦✦✦· ————

"Mein Damen und Herren, Mannheim Hauptbahnhof. Thank you for using Deutsch Bahn."

Snapped awake by the digital announcement Lars joins the line exiting the train.

He stops to buy a Fanta from a train station kiosk stocked with glossy magazines, international, and regional newspapers.

He sneers at the hated Tagblatt's latest issue.

Can in hand he passes rows of waiting taxis and overflowing bicycle racks, ducking under the welcome shade of a covered Strassenbahn stop.

———— ·✦✦✦✦· ————

## Mannheim Psychosomatic Medicine
## and Psychotherapy Department

"Guten tag Detective Kubach."

Lars accepts a handshake from a regal looking man wearing wire rimmed glasses.

A corded badge peeking under his blue hospital uniform identifies him as Doctor Karsten Schertz.

"Due to our new security regulations a doctor or nurse must escort all visitors. Please follow me to my office."

— ·•◆•· —

"How long did Doctor Kolb work here?" Lars asks.

"A year and a half, I didn't see him much. He worked the graveyard shift."

"Did he treat psychiatric cases?"

"Yes, he had ten patients. They were usually asleep when he came in, he had the night to himself."

"Do you have a list of names?"

"I'm sorry but such records are confidential, I cannot disclose them."

"Did he prescribe or give the patients any medicines?"

"Yes, but only the most severe cases."

"This might sound strange, but were there any patient deaths under his care?"

Schertz peers at Lars over his lowered glasses.

"I'm doing an investigation." Lars explains.

"We had one. A patient of his squeezed out an unlocked window and jumped from the fourth floor. When questioned by the Polizei, he was vague about the incident."

"Hmmm," Lars rubs his chin, "an unlocked window in a treatment facility for mental patients?"

"It's believed the patient may have worked it open over time. Anyway, an internal investigation found Doctor Kolb maintained poor records of the medicines he prescribed. Rather than be fired he submitted his resignation."

Shertz folds his hands in front of his chin.

"I hear Frankfurt has experienced some strange murders recently."

Lars clears his throat.

"Our investigation found that Doctor Kolb's medical credentials are suspicious. We are looking into whether the suspected killers were former patients of his."

Shertz's suspicious raised eyebrows tell Lars he has said too much.

He puts his notepad back in his shirt pocket.

"Thank you for your time, Herr Schertz."

# CHAPTER TWENTY-FIVE

## FRIDAY 9:30 A.M. LARS KUBACH'S OFFICE

AFTER A HALF HOUR SCROLLING through the *Mannheim Morgen's* archived news articles, Lars finds a headline.

⁺·⁺♦♦⁺·⁺

## DOCTOR FIRED FOR PRESCRIPTION ERRORS

A suicide investigation at the *Mannheim Mental Health Klinik* has led to a doctor's dismissal. The patient jumped from a fourth-floor window.

"One of the floor doctor's responsibilities is to check all windows. The doctor was found negligent and was released by mutual agreement. We express our condolences for this tragic incident and will help the family members through the grieving process." An anonymous hospital spokesperson said.

"We just want to know what happened to our son," the patient's mother said in a tearful interview. "He was due to be discharged in a week. It just doesn't seem like him."

Article saved; Lars accesses the Polizei case file.

INVESTIGATING OFFICER STATEMENT Case # 13359

*Doctor Victor Kolb states he performed his nightly bed check at the appropriate time (12 A.M.) and noticed nothing unusual in the patient's room. The patient, Juri Kellenhammer was said to be cooperative and well-mannered in most instances and was not considered a suicide risk. He exited a window above a narrow ledge. The window showed signs of tampering. A witness in the hospital parking lot stated he saw patient jump. Witness said he then rushed to the scene and found patient dead from massive head trauma. During questioning, Doctor Kolb displayed obvious signs of distress but had no explanation or cause for the incident. Patient had recently been prescribed a new experimental drug under the clinical name Halodan.*

+ + ✦ ✦ + +

"Halodan and another death." Lars mutters.

Hauptmann Muller's knock interrupts. He stalks inside, slamming the morning Tagblatt issue on the desk.

"What the hell is this all about?"

Lars rolls his eyes at the headline.

"Read it later, for now explain how it got out."

"Doctor Kolb apparently treated two of the killers. I met with his former employer."

"You went all the way to Mannheim? You couldn't just use the damn phone?"

"I never expected anyone to blab to the press."

"They did, and now Shurtzmann and I must explain this to the mayor tonight. What do you propose we tell her?"

"You could say the article is unconfirmed."

"Getting that tabloid to retract a juicy headline is near impossible. In fact, I expect them to dig deeper."

"I guess I'll take the heat for it."

Muller gives Lars a hot glare.

"I want something on my desk by four p.m."

He turns sharply and walks out.

His temples throbbing from a sudden headache Lars chases two Motrin with a sip of Gerolstiener mineral water.

---

## MURDERS LINKED TO DISGRACED DOCTOR?

*Frankfurt. - The wave of recent killings in Frankfurt may have a common thread. According to police sources two of the alleged killers were former patients of a doctor with a questionable past.*

*"The former doctor (name withheld) was fired for over-dispensing a controlled substance." admitted Doctor Karsten Schertz of Mannheim's prestigious Mental Health Klinik.*

*Halodan-the alleged prescribed medicine is a tightly monitored experimental treatment for mild paranoia and other forms of mental illness. When contacted about the doctor's certification to practice medicine, his current employer, the Saint Timothy Krankenhaus refused comment.*

Massaging his forehead, Lars keeps the sports page, jamming the other sections in his wastebasket.

---

## 1 P.M. SAINT TIMOTHY KRANKENHAUS

Smiling at Lars, the white-haired nurse rests her arms on the information desk counter.

"I'm sorry Herr officer but Doctor Kolb is not in, he works the night shift."

"I know but this is an urgent matter."

"I'll contact our on-call doctor. Please wait there."

A desk phone in one hand she points to a row of chairs in the lobby.

For thirty minutes Lars impatiently eyes the wall clock and a repeating hospital promotional video.

*A state-of-the-art trauma center...excellent mental and physical rehab services...eighty-room inpatient capacity...a refurbished cafeteria...and of course the smiling friendly staff...*

Arms folded; Doctor Andreas Fritsch curiously watches Lars thumbing through empty folders in Doctor Kolb's office file cabinet.

"We just learned about his past this morning." he says.

*No doubt from the fucking Tagblatt!*

"How well do you know him?" Lars asks.

"We talk occasionally. He works nights, kind of quiet, religious."

"You said religious?" Lars says without looking up.

"He didn't share it openly, but he was always reading the bible or religious tracts."

"Did he have an office computer?" Lars nods at a dust free circle on the desk.

"It may have been his personal one, I'm not sure."

Lars pulls the desk drawers open...scattered pens, paperclips, and a blank notebook.

"How many patients are under his care?"

"We have eight permanent and twelve outpatients. Doctor Kolb handled the most serious cases."

"Did he treat them with a drug called Halodan?"

"I am not at liberty to disclose that sir."

"I asked because he prescribed it to my brother."

"Oh, I am sorry about that. Doctor Kolb said Peter was often violent, but I never had any problems with him."

Lars opens a bi-fold closet door, feeling through the pockets of two lab coats and an old suit.

"It looks like he cleared out in a hurry. Are you sure he wasn't here this morning?" He says, his back turned.

"I can review the security cameras."

"Do that for me please."

"If you don't mind, Herr Kubach, this whole fake doctor thing, we don't want a scandal to grow until we can figure out what to do."

"Any more than we do. All we want is to find him."

Fritsch looks both ways down the hall, he closes the door and lowers his voice.

"I can get his address."

<hr />

## 2:15 P.M.

"Doctor Kolb turned in his keys and left early this morning."

Lars follows Doctor Kolb's landlord down a bare floored freshly painted hallway.

"I'm sorry about the smell but I'm doing renovations. Had to remove the carpeting too."

"Thank you, Herr Rau, for your cooperation on such short notice, what can you tell me about him?"

"Not much, we never really talked. He left every evening at the same time to catch the strassenbahn."

"He had no car?"

Herr Rau shakes his head.

Lars opens the refrigerator.

"Still food inside." He says flatly.

Herr Rau peeks in and nods.

"You're sure he's not coming back?" Lars asks.

"Yes, he paid the balance due and told my receptionist to keep the security deposit."

Lars rummages through a dresser full of folded underwear, balls of socks, and undershirts.

"Was he carrying anything?"

"Just a gym bag."

"Any regular visitors?"

"No sir to be honest he really wasn't here a lot."

Sliding open a closet door, Lars parts a row of shirts on hangers; a booklet drops to the floor.

*The Judgment Seat.*

Crouching down he deftly slides it up his sleeve.

Herr Rau peers over his shoulder.

"Is something wrong?"

"We just want to talk with him. Thank you for your time, Herr Rau."

———— ·+◆◆◆+· ————

## 3:50 P.M. BAHNHOFSVIERTEL STATION

*Hallo Manfred, I need Doctor Kolb's patient lists from St. Timothy Krankenhaus and Mannheim Mental Health Klinik.*

Lars clicks send on his hastily typed email.

Peter's shimmering face suddenly flashes on the monitor, followed by a series of grisly microsecond images.

*Matthias Hinkel's shattered skull…*

*Hans Neubauer's destroyed eye socket…*

*Detlef Bergmeyer's mouth of smashed teeth…*

His trembling hand picks up his ringing office phone.

"Guten tag Herr Detective, Doctor Fritsch here. I reviewed the security tape. Doctor Kolb arrived at eleven with a gym bag. He left with the same bag at eleven fifty."

*An hour before I got there–damn.*

"Thank you doctor Fritsch."

His eyes dart to the wall clock.

*Five minutes. Scheisse!*

Tucking his case folder under his arm he gulps down his now cold coffee and hurriedly locks his office.

# CHAPTER TWENTY-SIX

## HAUPTMANN MULLER'S OFFICE

"**Y**OU'RE LATE. HAVE A SEAT."

"Sorry sir. Here are my case notes."

Muller slowly flips through them-stopping randomly to read.

He leans back in his chair, arms folded.

"I'm curious about something, how did you discover Doctor Kolb's fake credentials?"

"I did some digging."

"I admit this is strange, but I thought you were looking into a cult."

"I still am, but this is related to the case. As I highlighted, Doctor Kolb has a history of prescribing an experimental medication with bad side effects. That-and his fake credentials make him worth looking into."

"Halodan is a recognized drug for depression and mental issues. This evidence is circumstantial and based on inference."

"How so sir? Each killer had traces in their system."

"True, but deliberate intent on his part is hard to prove. All he has to say is that he prescribes the medicine. What a patient does after that is beyond him."

"Sir, two of his patients, including my brother committed suicide after he prescribed them Halodan. He also prescribed it to Detlef Bergmeyer and treated Matthias Hinkel. That's four people dead.

Considering his hasty departure, he's obviously on the run from something."

Muller stands up, hands in his pockets he paces behind his desk.

"I think the Tagblatt article spooked him. If anything, it's to avoid arrest for medical fraud."

"Or a connection with brother Enoch."

Muller stops Lars with a raised palm.

"Wait a minute. You can't be serious. Based on what evidence?"

"I found a religious tract in his apartment similar the one Detlef Bergmeyer had."

"That's hardly enough to draw such a conclusion."

"Admittedly yes but the connection is possible."

Muller takes a deep breath.

"You really believe this cult thing, don't you?"

"I just need time to connect it with Doctor Kolb."

Muller slowly shakes his head.

"Look Lars, time is not a luxury right now. The media claims we are a city under siege. The mayor wants something plausible in time for the weekend news cycle. Three obviously troubled killers can be readily explained as coincidental."

"Only for so long. The drug angle is already out."

"Thanks to you." Muller snaps.

"Well than there is your answer. Avoid negative publicity at all costs, using stall tactics."

Muller slams his palms on his desk.

"I have to stall because you are busy chasing ghost leads! Get out there and solve this goddamn case! Now excuse me but I'm running late, Shurtzmann is waiting for me at the mayor's office."

He pushes the case folder across his desk and dismissively waves Lars to the door.

---

## 8:30 P.M.

His engine and lights off, Lars watches Brother Enoch's apartment across the street.

Headlights flash in his side mirror.

Lowering his Eintracht Frankfurt hat, he slides down.

Nigel Trotter's white van glides past and parks.

Lars peeks over his dashboard.

Nigel looks briefly around, opens the waist high ornamental sidewalk gate and disappears behind a border hedge.

Lars softly clicks his door shut.

A walker in the murky twilight-he leisurely drifts past the gate.

Pretending to tie his shoe he stoops beside Nigel's van and pulls out his information card with a penned message on the back.

*'Meet me, pick a place.'*

A dog yaps in the distance.

*It's Oliver! Scheisse!*

With one eye on Giselle Rosenblatt's rapid approach, he hastily slides his card under Nigel's wiper blade.

Back turned, his hat lowered, he briskly strides to the Saab, getting inside just as she strolls past.

*"Good she didn't notice me."*

A silhouetted figure on the second floor slides the curtain back a sliver, watching him drive away.

# CHAPTER TWENTY-SEVEN

SHIELDED FROM THE ARID MIDDAY sun by a sidewalk café's fluttering parasol, Lars reads the *Frankfurter Tagblatt's* front page article.

## NO LINK BETWEEN DRUG AND VIOLENCE

*Frankfurt. – An experimental drug for depression and paranoia may not be a factor in two recent slayings as first believed. Manufactured under the brand name Halodan, the drug corrects neurotransmitter imbalances in the brain.*

*"Halodan is essentially a mood-altering drug, but I must stress that there is no conclusive evidence linking it to violent behavior. Rigorous testing has proven it effective for treating depression. To blame it for murder or suicide is pure speculation and totally unwarranted. However as with any drug, abuse may have undesirable consequences." A WaldBrunner spokesperson said yesterday.*

————◆◆◆◆◆————

"Tell my brother that you liars."

He slaps the paper on the grated metal table.

Sipping a mineral water, he scans Kaiserstrasse's bustling Saturday crowd.

Teenagers' heads down, walking and texting...outdoor café tables filled with people eating and drinking...and passing men stealing glances at Oom leaving the *Mumbai Café* carrying two sandwiches.

+ + + ♦ + + +

"Thank you for lunch." she says biting into an overstuffed Doner Kebab.

Still chewing, she reaches in the two handled shopping bag Lars has been guarding.

He lowers his reddening face as she inventories the contents from *NYMPHOS Sex Shop.*

*Ankle high stiletto boots, sheer red and black teddies, a body stocking, a shiny leather corset.*

"Not all for my workers. Maybe I wear *this* for you."

She winks, holding up a glossy black latex cat suit.

His eyes widening, Lars spots a Volkswagen T-5 slowing to a crawl.

"Put that away!" He hisses at Oom.

A face half hidden by a camera leans out the rolled down passenger window.

"Hey! He take a picture. Did you see that?"

The van backs into a vacant parking spot.

"Him again," Lars mutters. "It's the media."

Oom stuffs the catsuit in the bag and quickly wraps her half-eaten Kebab.

She lowers her sunglasses off her forehead and rises from her chair. "Let's go."

"Too late, I'll intercept them." Lars says.

Frizzy hair and his trailing cameraman strut to the table.

"Detective Kubach do you have any comments on the recent murders?"

"No, we were just leaving. We're in a hurry if you don't mind."

Frizzy hair subtly nods to his cameraman.

"I'm sorry are we interrupting something?"

Oom grabs the bag and sandwich, her face turned, she briskly leaves the table followed closely by Lars.

Matching their strides, frizzy hair catches up to them.

Lars holds up a palm.

"Please no cameras."

"Are the stories about Doctor Kolb true?"

"No comment."

"Is he a suspect?"

"No comment."

Brushing past Lars, frizzy hair jabs a voice recorder toward Oom.

"Miss, are you the Eros Sauna's owner?"

"No comment."

Oom swishes her hair over her shoulder and picks up her pace.

"Leave her out of this." Lars says tersely.

The cameraman focuses on the cat suit leg dangling from Oom's bag.

Lars steps between them, shielding the lens with his palm.

"Look I said no cameras."

"Is that part of your investigation?"

Arching his eyebrows frizzy hair smirks at the bag.

"That's it." Lars hisses, his fists clenching.

Oom cuts between them, tightly gripping the bag, she strains to body block Lars.

Passing faces turn to look; feeling multiple stares Lars stiffly stalks off fumbling for his car keys.

"Get a life." he shouts over his shoulder.

Parked outside Oom's apartment, Lars pulls down his visor to block the blinding sun.

Next to him Oom packs a joint.

"I guess we're a celebrity couple now."

"Ohh…I always want to be famous." Oom giggles.

Holding the joint to her lips, she seductively licks the glue.

Lars looks at her sideways with a pinched frown.

"You know I could bust you."

She grins, lights it and puffs, marijuana smoke spirals out the passenger window.

"You want try it?"

Lars looks at her sideways.

"Fuck it give it here."

———— ·+·♦♦·+· ————

Glassy eyed, mouth agape, Lars leans back on his headrest blankly examining the Saab's roof.

"You are first time smoker?" Oom asks between coughs.

"A few times in school." He mumbles.

Oom flicks the glowing remnant out the window.

"Muller gave me soccer tickets do you want to go?"

"Yes, Frankfurt better than Thai team."

"Don't be too sure about that."

Lars chuckles, turning to her with a dreamy stare.

"Your eyes are really red." She says.

"Well, your nose is cute."

"No, it's wide like a bus."

They cough and laugh in spasms.

Oom pushes her sandals off her feet; she rests her head on his shoulder.

Parting a hair strand from her face, he kisses her forehead.

"You said something about a catsuit?" He whispers.

# CHAPTER TWENTY-EIGHT

## TWO A.M.

"Tonight, young man you will hear the power of God."

Brother Enoch paternally pats his studio visitor's shoulder.

He adjusts his headphones and pulls his microphone close.

"Greetings listeners, Jahweh's word says there were sodomites in the land that did abominations in defiance of his holy law. There are sodomites in the land today. They defile themselves with man as Ham did when he took advantage of his father Noah's drunkenness."

"Leviticus eighteen twenty-two says to lie with a man like a woman is an abomination, and chapter twenty, verse thirteen says that if a man lies with another man, they both have committed abomination and they shall surely be put to death. Deuteronomy twenty-two five says it is an abomination for a woman to wear men's clothes and a man to wear woman's clothes."

"But today we see the butches and lesbians wearing jeans and assuming male roles and drag queens and those claiming to be the wrong sex and changing that which Jahweh has given them!"

"Ladies and gentlemen, these abominations are taking place right now! Men have left the natural use of the woman and burned in their lust for each other, men with men to the point where Jahweh has given them a reprobate mind!"

"They are unashamed they don't blush instead they declare their sin like Sodom. The militant homosexual movement is boldly in our face. They defy Jahweh, pushing for equality and same sex unions that threaten the sanctity of traditional marriage."

"In Matthew nineteen Jesus gave the Pharisees a *straight* answer about marriage. He said a man will leave his parents to be with his wife and they shall be one. The command is clear. What Jahweh has joined let no man dissolve. Relationships and marriage belong to a man and a woman not two men or two women! Gayness is a genetic defect, the result of fallen sinners handed down through generations after the flood. They even hijacked the rainbow, a sign of Jahweh's covenant to mock him!"

Brother Enoch turns, smiling at his guest.

"The men of Sodom were wicked and sinners before God, giving themselves to fornication, going after strange flesh. Some say Frankfurt's sins rival those of Sodom. I say they are worse and have reached unto heaven! These modern sodomites are everywhere in this metropolis of sin. They are after our children and our families. The righteous are besieged at every corner and now that gays think they need rights nothing shall restrain them."

"But there was one righteous man in Sodom named Lot who vexed his soul daily at their filthy conversation and unlawful deeds. Lot was so distressed that he offered his own daughters to rabid homosexuals so depraved they wanted to sleep with the visiting angels! And now we offer our children to schools that teach them to accept alternative lifestyles. But what happened? The angels blinded the men and Jahweh rained fire and brimstone on the two cities, saving only Lot and his two daughters. And unless Jahweh again finds a very small remnant, we will suffer the vengeance of eternal fire like them. Today we are that remnant that vexes their souls and prays for deliverance! Jahweh has called us to cleanliness and holiness. Those hearing *this prophet's* voice cease from your lusts and fornications and adulteries lest you be consumed."

"Therefore, I say to the effeminate and abusers of themselves with mankind and filthy dreamers that defile the flesh *you* shall not inherit the kingdom."

"God's wrath is revealed from heaven! He will pour out his fury upon you! He will judge you according to *your* ways and repay you for your abominations! The apostle Paul said to mark them which cause divisions and offences. Jahweh commands us like the king of Judah to break down the houses of the Sodomites, and to smite them in the same manner. Jesus told Peter to put up his sword, but he has told me the second Enoch to keep it sharp! I am anointed to fulfill his word. I am a righteous holy prophet and for a good man some would even dare to die, therefore offer your body as a living sacrifice. Go and prepare the way of the Lord, Amen, and goodnight until next time."

Headphones off, Enoch turns to his visitor.

"Young man, prepare the way of the Lord."

# CHAPTER TWENTY-NINE

## NOON: SUNDAY

IS HEART RACING AFTER A flurry of boxing combinations on his heavy bag, Lars towels off his sweaty forehead.

He opens his apartment balcony's sliding glass door and stares up admiring the cloudless soaring ocean blue sky.

He stops tying his running shoes to read a new text.

*"Lars it's Officer Detweiler, I just got a call about a protest at Club Bacchus."*

## *PINK PLATZ*: FRANKFURT'S GAY SECTION

Still in his Eintracht Frankfurt track suit, Lars parks behind Detweiler's Polizei cruiser.

Across the street a neon pink lettered *Club Bacchus* sign flashes above the bar's red felt covered door.

Multi-colored blinking rope lights frame a tinted picture window covered with large pictures of smiling muscular bare-chested men.

The same women from the Eros Sauna protest silently march back and forth on the sidewalk carrying different signs this time.

*AIDS: the Eleventh plague*
*Sodom and Gomorrah equal Sodomy and Gonorrhea*
The stork proudly totes the largest sign.
**GAY**: *God Against You*

Two new faces march with them, Brother Enoch's buzz cut keyboardist, and a gaunt faced youth in faded jeans and a short sleeve shirt carrying a *Martyr for Jahweh* sign.

Staying low behind his steering wheel, Lars furtively snaps pictures of their faces.

An approaching group of obviously gay counter protesters march past the Saab blocking his view.

More signs...

*Hate free zone!*

*Fix marriage not gays!*

*Two pairs beat a straight*

The counter protesters line up linking arms in front of Club Bacchus.

Two beefy muscled bouncers join them in a loud chant.

*"Stay away if you're not gay...Stay away if you're not gay..."*

Their chants and taunts grow louder each time the two young men shuffle past.

A balding man in black leather pants and a mesh tank top blows an exaggerated mock kiss at the gaunt youth.

"Hi pretty boy drink a beer with a queer?" He says leering at him with a fingertip wave.

A flash in his side mirror distracts Lars-the *Tagblatt* van backing into a parking spot.

*Damn when does this guy sleep?*

Sunk down hoping frizzy hair or his driver won't spot the Saab, he sighs with relief at flashing lights from a Polizei van stopping in the middle of the street.

Slamming doors, four officers in flak vests stride with military precision toward the two groups.

The driver leans out the van window with a megaphone.

"This protest is now over. You have five minutes to peaceably leave. I repeat you have five minutes."

Driving slowly through the disbanding groups, Lars grins widely at frizzy hair's frustrated face in his rearview mirror.

"No story today asshole."

Free from the crowd, he laughs and speeds off.

―――――・・◆◆◆・・―――――

## Monday Morning: Lars Kubach's office

His radio tuned to Hessischer Rundfunk Lars listens to an interview while adjusting his tie in his computer screen.

*"What about reports of Halodan's dangerous side effects?"*

*"They are unconfirmed. Halodan is completely safe when taken as prescribed."*

*"So, it doesn't cause violent irrational behavior?"*

*"Attempts to connect it with the recent deaths are without merit. The killers had documented unstable histories."*

*"What can you tell us about the doctor?"*

*"That is a hospital matter I'm not at liberty to comment."*

*"Thank you for your time, sir."*

*"Thank you."*

*"That was an exclusive interview with WaldBrunner spokesman Walther Huer...and now the latest news..."*

Rolling his eyes, Lars turns off the radio and answers his ringing cell phone.

"Guten Morgen Lars, I accessed Doctor Kolb's patient files, I have a list of eight patients under his care."

Imagining Schollner's proud smile on the other end, Lars starts making his morning coffee.

"Can you match the names to faces?"

"I'll run them through. I will email what I find."

―――――・・◆◆◆・・―――――

## AN HOUR LATER:

Sipping coffee, Lars studies the faces on his computer screen.

Three are familiar, Matthias Hinkel, Detlef Bergmeyer, and-he looks away from the screen, biting his lip.

*My brother.*

Two other faces match his Club Bacchus snapshots.

"Hermann Renke, and Gunnar Weiss, Brother Enoch's keyboard player."

He brings up Doctor Kolb's patient list, scrolling through admission and discharge dates.

"Five in outpatient status, one redacted name and one under permanent care."

The far-right column lists each patient's case worker.

Lars stops suddenly his hand cupped over his mouth.

"Wait a minute! Five patients referred by Nigel Trotter! Oh my god! Doctor Kolb, Nigel Trotter, and the cult are connected!"

# CHAPTER THIRTY

## *Saint Timothy Krankenhaus* Mental Ward

"HE'S IN THE RECREATION ROOM."

"Don't mention I am a detective." Lars says with a chuckle.

"There he is."

Lars follows the orderly's directed eyes to a young man lining up a shot on a pool table.

He has a former meth addict's sunken cheeks and dark eye circles-as the orderly warned Lars in the hallway.

"Hello Kurt, this is mister Kubach, he wants to talk to you."

Kurt places his pool stick in a notched rack.

"Just wait until I get back." he says randomly.

Lars and the orderly exchange a sideways look.

Kurt greets Lars with a vigorous handshake.

"I am Kurtis Adler. The best pool player here."

The orderly confirms with a nod.

"Good for you Kurtis. Do you recognize this man?"

Kurt squints at the photo Lars holds up.

"That's Mister Trotter."

"What can you tell me about him?"

"Are you a spy?" Kurt blurts out.

The orderly looks away hiding a faint grin.

"No Kurt, I assure you I am no spy."

"He's clean." Kurt whispers over his shoulder.

"Who are you talking to?" Lars asks.

"My partner, we play pool every day. He's joining the Bundeswehr soon."

"I see…" Lars scans the empty room.

The beet red orderly turns and leaves.

"Mister Trotter is a nice guy." Kurt blurts out.

"How so?"

"He sent me here to protect me from the devil."

"Are you scared of the devil?"

Kurt shakes his head vigorously.

"Not anymore. My medicine keeps him away."

"Who gives you the medicine?"

"My doctor."

"What's your doctor's name?"

"Doctor Kolb."

"Is he a nice guy too?"

"Yes, he says Jesus can beat the devil."

"He talks with you about God?"

Kurt looks over his shoulder at the stick rack.

"I don't want to talk no more my partner is waiting."

"Ok, thank you Kurtis."

---

"I told you," The orderly whispers in the hallway. "He has acute paranoia."

"Does Doctor Kolb visit him?"

"Once a week on Saturday."

"And mister Trotter?"

"Not since Doctor Kolb told him Kurtis was admitted as a permanent patient."

"*They* talked?"

"Oh yeah kinda like they knew each other."

"Did mister Trotter meet any of the other patients?"

"I saw him here a few times."

"Do you know if he counseled them as well?"

"I believe so. Doctor Kolb said some of them were making enough progress to be released."

"Really? Did he say into whose custody or care?"

"I didn't ask, but I overheard a halfway house-um I think it was the Klaus... Moritz... Ubergangszentrum?"

The orderly presses the elevator down button.

His face turning pale, Lars rides in silence.

"Are you ok sir?"

"Yes, I'm just thinking. Did the families have any say in these decisions?"

"As far as I know they were ok with it."

"That's strange."

"You see a lot of strange things here sir." The orderly says as the elevator bumps to a stop.

+·+·✦·✦·+·+·


## MONDAY EVENING

Sipping Maisel's Weisse in his usual Kaiser Bistro barstool, Lars scans the *Frankfurter TagBlatt* headlines.

**Train Surfing, A new most dangerous game?**

**Eagles changing defensive scheme after another loss.**

**Airport Worker: "We had orders to profile travelers."**

He angrily stares at the last headline and a photo of him and Oom at the Mumbai Café.

"That rotten bastard." He mutters.

+·+·✦·✦·+·+·

## Detective's Secret Love Tryst?

*Frankfurt – As preparations begin for Frankfurt's annual Museumsuferfest, a crime wave has the city under siege.*

*A tourist robbing African gang has turned increasingly violent and an investigation into a series of bizarre murders has stalled. To find answers we attempted to interview lead detective Lars Kubach. Tersely rebuffing questions, he became belligerent and had to be restrained from attacking our cameraman.*

*His companion is identified as Oom Suthaparn current proprietor of the Eros Sauna–the scene of socialite Gabrielle Mecklenburg's slaying three weeks ago.*

*An anonymous source revealed Frau Mecklenburg was investigated last year for a marriage citizenship scandal.*

*Volunteer German nationals were paid up to five thousand Euros to file fraudulent marriage documents allowing foreigners to obtain work and resident permits.*

*The elaborate scheme included fake wedding pictures and shared chat messages on social network sites.*

*Some of the men never met their brides. The scam unraveled when an illegal worker was found in the massage parlor during a routine inspection.*

*Frau Mecklenburg faced visa and marriage fraud charges. In an unusual move they were dropped without further inquiry. Oom Suthaparn was married and was allegedly involved in the scam.*

Lars slaps the paper on the counter, drawing scattered looks from fellow drinkers.

He holds up his empty glass, his usual refill signal.

His cell phone buzzes–an incoming text.

*In my office 10 A.M.*

"Fuck this." He yells, attracting more stares.

---

His forehead beaded with sweat Lars holds up the Tagblatt's front page.

"Is this true?"

Oom snatches the paper and tosses it on her sofa.

"I don't want to talk about."

"Well, I do. Why didn't I know about this?"

"You no ask me." Her voice trails from the kitchen.

"I shouldn't have to. I thought we trust each other."

She returns handing him an open Spezi.

"How do I know *you* are here legally?" he asks after a gulp.

"You are a Polizei, go check."

"Maybe I should. And you're high again. I smelled it when I came in."

"So what? I smell beer too. You drunk to face problems, me..." she points to herself. "Relax and think."

"I just want the truth. About you and about us."

"Truth? Okay I tell you. Frau M arrange marriage for me for Visa and work permit, then she makes me assistant."

"Then she *was* guilty? Why wasn't she charged?"

"I say nothing more, the paper already said."

"It also said you were involved."

Her face tightening Oom paces the room, she stops- glaring at Lars.

"You arrest me?" She defiantly holds out her arms palms up.

"What the hell's wrong with you today?" Lars shouts.

"What's wrong? I lose money and customers. Some girls quit and no new ones want to work for Sauna. Now this news headline. I am sick of it!"

"You could have told me you were married."

"I not married anymore."

"It doesn't matter now."

Lars drains the Spezi and takes out his car keys.

"You are leaving me?"

"I need time to think about us."

"Take time, go on get out!"

Stomping barefooted, she yanks the door open and waves at him to go.

# CHAPTER THIRTY-ONE

USING THE CLEAREST SHOT FROM frizzy hair's protest interview, Lars isolates and crops the stork's face.

He enters the scanned image on his computer and waits, yawning and rubbing his bleary red eyes.

Hundreds of images later, he has a match.

"So, she does have a name."

He takes a bite of his breakfast, a cream cheese filled Brötchen and turns up *ZDF Morgenmagazin*.

*"Are the accusations against Doctor Kolb meritless?" the interviewer asks.*

*A suited man straightens up in his chair.*

*"We are certain he did not improperly administer Halodan to any of his patients." He says stiffly.*

*"Are you aware of reports that he was fired from his previous job?"*

*"Yes." The man says with irritated curtness.*

*"So how he was hired here in Frankfurt?"*

*His cheeks flushing the man straightens his tie.*

*"All applications…are thoroughly screened before a hiring decision is made."*

*"But is it possible that Doctor Kolb's invalid credentials were overlooked?"*

*"It's possible and he is on a leave of absence pending further internal investigation."*

*"Thank you, for your time Herr Freur."*

The split screen switches back to the news anchor facing the camera.

*"That was Saint Timothy Krankenhaus director Wilhelm Freur. In other news, the Frankfurt Eros Sauna was raided late last night. Police say the owner is accused of sex trafficking."*

His mouth open, Lars watches a video feed of flashing police lights and two grim faced officers leading a handcuffed Oom from the Eros Sauna.

"Damn it! She's going to think I did that!"

⋅᛫᛭᛭᛭᛫⋅

## TEN A.M. HAUPTMANN MULLER'S OFFICE

Hauptmann Muller closes the case folder and rests his crossed arms on his desk.

"If Doctor Kolb was fired in Mannheim, how did he find work here without red flags popping up?"

"That's what I can't figure out sir, but I found some interesting things on his patient list."

"Explain." Hauptmann Muller says with a sighing yawn.

"An expat social worker named Nigel Trotter referred five young men to him, all within the last year and a half. One of them was Detlef Bergmeyer."

Muller reopens the case folder flipping to a page.

"I also see Matthias Hinkel and a redacted name, both referred by two different social workers, where do they fit in?"

"I just received the list, so I haven't had time to check on them, but what's curious is that all of Nigel Trotter's referrals except Kurtis Adler were treated for three months and released as outpatients."

"Ninety days is common for most mental patients."

"True, however one of them-Gunnar Weiss, is brother Enoch's keyboardist. The other is identified as Herman Renke, both were at Sunday's Club Bacchus protest."

"Are you serious?"

"Yes sir. It took some work, but I contacted their families by phone yesterday. They refused to say anything other than they signed release papers agreeing to outpatient therapy."

"Do the families know about this Enoch character?"

"They were evasive when I asked but said they were satisfied with their sons' progress and claimed they were doing well."

"Both families said the same thing?"

"Yes sir, almost as if reading from a script."

"Let me play devil's advocate. Could this brother Enoch simply be ministering to troubled youths?"

"I saw no signs of that. Nigel Trotter currently works as a shelter youth counselor. I've seen his van frequently parked at the cult's address."

"You're kidding?"

His eyebrows arching, Muller reexamines the list.

"No sir, and one other thing, I spent hours late last night comparing pictures in our facial recognition system."

"Pictures of who?"

"The building owner, Marianna Obermayer is a cult member. She was a nurse's aide for two years at Nuremburg's *Friedrich Mansfield Health Center* and currently an order processor for *Deutschland Novelties and Souvenir Exports*. Her work history is too short and neither job would pay enough for her to buy the building outright."

"Money laundering?"

"I'm not ruling that out. Not long-ago Brother Enoch was a street preacher, now he has a shortwave broadcast and an entire apartment building serving as a church, I doubt he gets enough member donations to sustain all that."

"It seems you are on to something here, but I still wonder if this is just what it looks like, a pastor and a counselor failing to help troubled persons."

"Sir, how can you dismiss Doctor Kolb? He is connected as well. I have Detlef Bergmeyer's prescription bottle with his name on it."

Muller releases a drawn-out sigh.

"And that's why I wanted you here. Shurtzmann called me late last night from Mayor Hagen's office. A *Waldbrunner* executive was there. He's blaming **you** for demonizing Halodan and causing the potential loss of future sales."

"Perhaps he should blame the company website. The drug's side effects are there for anyone to read."

"Whatever, but Shurtzmann wants you to drop the drug theory."

"A pharmaceutical company's dipping profits are more important than murderers using one of their drugs?"

Muller rises from his chair like a cobra, he leans forward, both arms braced on his desk.

"Enough! As I said that angle is finished."

"Sir, this is the second time he's left a hospital after a patient death over Halodan. What happens if he gets another job, more strange deaths?"

"Look, if you persist, I'll pull you from this case. Do you understand?"

His eyes narrowed, Lars nods with clenched teeth.

Ignoring his flushed glare, Muller turns and pours water in his coffee maker.

He sighs to calm himself.

"Listen, Heaven's Gate, Jim Jones, David Koresh, we don't need those names associated with our city. And now you're adding a killer doctor. My guess is he won't be coming back, and without stronger evidence we can't do much. It seems more prudent to keep an eye on the outpatients, and it might be wise to find out more about this Trotter character."

His back still turned; Muller refills his empty mug.

Holding it waist high he sits back down.

"We're not done yet. Now, about your little friend, you should know most of her workers are here illegally."

"Go on." Lars snaps, correctly guessing Muller's next words.

"The article about you socializing with her and her arrest doesn't look good for your investigation."

"It was an off-record interview."

"Oh really? She's facing pandering and attempted blackmail charges."

"Blackmail? What are you talking about?"

"Apparently her employees think they can make threats about going public with details of a scandal."

"What kind of scandal?"

"One of them left messages with the desk Sergeant claiming an officer raped her at a party Sunday night, she said she will expose all client names unless she gets paid. Were you aware of this?"

"No sir I wasn't."

"That jackass Tagblatt reporter already suspects a ledger. We don't need some whore contacting him about writing her memoirs and naming names."

"So you arrest Oom hoping to shut her up?"

"All Oom has to do is cooperate."

"Cooperate how?"

"Look-we need to know if this ledger is real or not."

Lars throws up his hands and shakes his head.

"This is really unnecessary."

"You want unnecessary?" Muller thrusts his chin at his door. "Lock it and we'll talk."

Hands in his pockets, he paces behind his desk.

"Your little buddy is already in the spotlight because of the murder at her brothel. We need assurance she won't blow this up as well."

"Thereby avoiding another scandal, I get it, let me talk with her."

"I will consider it, but one thing remains."

Head down Muller releases a resigned sigh.

"Due to your recent temper exhibitions and loss of your brother I have been urged to recommend you for stress management counseling. You need to make an appointment immediately."

# CHAPTER THIRTY-TWO

## ONE P.M. LARS KUBACH'S OFFICE

EROTIC IMAGES OF A BIKINI clad Oom gyrating on a Bangkok bar stage vanish when the Standesamt records clerk takes Lars off hold.

"I'm sorry detective but there is no marriage certificate for an Oom South..a..porn."

"Suthaparn," Lars corrects him, "are there any other records?"

"There is a divorce decree from a Werner Musselman."

"Do you have further information about him?"

"Herr Musselman is fifty years old he was born in Ludwigshafen. He was a Lufthansa travel agent for fifteen years before relocating to Thailand as a German language teacher and interpreter."

"Thank you, for your time sir." Lars says.

His cell phone chirps, he checks the text.

*Ying's China Palace 6 p.m. Nigel*

---

## EVENING: DOWNTOWN FRANKFURT

*Ying's China Palace* is a brief walk from the Hauptbahnhof to Kaiserstrasse.

The dinnertime crowd is a mixed lot–an obvious banker finished for the day, a tired faced woman shushing two whining toddlers, and a raucous chattering tourist group–Australian according to the flags sewn on most of their backpacks.

The noise and ambient music drown out Das Erste's news-which Lars has given up watching.

At exactly six, an impeccably dressed silver haired man enters, letting in a gust of humid evening air.

His roaming grey eyes find Lars.

"Guten Abend. I'm Deacon Nigel Trotter, or Brother Aaron." He says in English accented German.

Lars looks up from his phone. Smiling uneasily, he offers a handshake.

"It's nice to meet you sir."

"How could I resist after such a covert contact method? James Bond would certainly be jealous."

Lars chuckles. "Dinner is on me sir."

"Thank you, I see we are in the smoking section, do you mind if I smoke?"

"No sir."

"It's a sin I battle with." he says with a sly grin.

Taking a scarlet pack of classic Davidoff's from his dress shirt pocket he taps out a cigarette, lighting it with an embossed silver Zippo.

The rising smoke curls around his wrinkled leathery face, accented by a neatly clipped grey mustache.

*A face less wrinkled on his driver license…*

"I am a spiritual advisor, are you seeking guidance?" he says.

"No sir I am an investigator. I just have some questions. I understand you are also a youth counselor at the *Klaus Moritz Uberganzentrum?*"

Nigel turns, slowly exhaling a billowing bluish cloud.

"I work as a counselor yes."

"What can you tell me about Detlef Bergmeyer?"

Nigel stubs the cigarette butt in an ash tray, he immediately lights another.

"He did occasional volunteer work at the center." He says between puffs.

"Did you interact with him or counsel him at all?"

"He was a troubled young man. I had a few chats with him...when he did show up."

"Did he ever mention his family?"

"Not at all, from what I gathered he was a drifter."

Lars leans close, lowering his voice.

"I asked because I'm looking for a motive. Were there warning signs he would do such a crime?"

His lips pursed Nigel shakes his head.

"None at all, in fact I was shocked like everyone else. I felt bad that perhaps I could have prevented the tragedy."

Nigel takes a longer puff, looking reflective.

*A little too exaggerated.*

"He did have one strange habit..."

A waitress interrupts, handing them laminated menu cards, and two courtesy bottles of mineral water.

She waits silently while they decide.

Lars points to a picture of shrimp fried rice.

"I'll have number five."

"And for me the orange chicken." Nigel says.

She bows, takes the menu cards and hurries to another table.

"Now, where were we? Oh yes, the lad always carried a backpack and seemed obsessed with keeping it arranged."

"That's a start, is there anything else?"

Nigel flashes a cryptic smile.

"He did confess that a male brothel owner abused him."

Recalling images of the obese *Inuus Lauf Haus* manager Lars scrunches his face.

"Did he say how long it went on?"

"No, but perhaps in his angry twisted mind he went after someone he thought he could handle?"

Nigel's eyebrows tilt suggestively.

"That's a detail I will have to check. He was treated as an outpatient by a Doctor Victor Kolb, do you know him?"

"I'm not aware of that name."

*Got him! He's lying.*

"One last question, did a young man named Petr Nowak ever visit the center?"

Nigel taps out another cigarette from his pack.

His hand quivers as he lights it.

"He did but I haven't seen him for a few weeks." He says through a puff.

*Another lie?*

"What can you tell me about him?"

"I never counseled him but I can say he is depressed due to lack of work, so we assist him and let him use our address to look for jobs."

"Are you referring to the church if you don't mind my asking?"

"Our church does provide help beyond a spiritual nature yes."

Nigel's relieved eyes dart to the approaching waitress.

She sets down their plates and rushes to two suited men taking their seats.

"Is Petr in some sort of trouble?" Nigel asks after a sip of water.

"No, but his name appeared in our database."

"Hmmm, well after all he is a little strange."

Nigel winks and stabs a piece of orange glazed chicken with his fork.

# CHAPTER THIRTY-THREE

## Late evening: Lars Kubach's apartment

"*H*is EYEBROWS ARE DIFFERENT, AND *he has more wrinkles, it's not him. I just know it.*"

Still holding Nigel Trotter's German license, Lars reviews his emails and clicks send.

---

To: *London University* Student Records Department.
From: Detective Lars Kubach, Polizei district Four,
Frankfurt am Main.
Subject: Request for records

*I am requesting information on Nigel Trotter a former student currently residing in Frankfurt Germany. My contact number is included in an attachment. Office hours: 0730 – 1700 local time. Thank you. Detective Lars Kubach*

---

"*Herr Schollner. Hi old friend. I am looking for information on an English expat named Nigel Trotter. He's not in our database except for a German class B license. Attached is what I have so far.*"

He logs off, turns on his shortwave and adjusts the antenna for the best reception to Brother Enoch's broadcast.

---

*"In the book of Ezekiel Jahweh showed him women weeping for Tammuz and priests worshipping the sun in the inner court and said you will see greater abominations than these. Ladies and gentlemen Jahweh's words have come to pass. Every day, men file in and out of brothels and sex shows. But the greatest abomination is the radical homosexual agenda being forced on the world; they wish to exterminate Jahweh's followers so they may continue to live unhindered in sin. We the righteous dwell among an unclean people. Their sins are open, and they follow the path of other sinners."*

*"Because of their ignorance and the blindness of their hearts Jahweh has blocked their understanding and refused them from the kingdom of heaven. These double minded sinners are beyond feeling, they glorify their shameful actions and lewdness. But take heart ye faithful, they shall not inherit god's kingdom. God is not mocked! His wrath is revealed from heaven against all ungodliness and sin and their end will be destruction!"*

*"We are not to pray for their souls, we are not to love the sinner and hate the sin! The book of Enoch declares, those who build their houses with sin shall be overthrown. And those who acquire gold and silver in judgment shall suddenly perish. Fear not the sinners, ye righteous, for the lord will deliver them into your hands, that ye may execute judgment upon them according to your desires."*

Brother Enoch's voice drops to a serious whisper.

*"And their judgment can no longer wait..."*

# CHAPTER THIRTY-FOUR

## AFRICAN GANG STRIKES AGAIN

*B*AHNHOFSVIERTEL. — FOR THE SECOND *time in a week a tourist was robbed at knifepoint by a suspected African gang operating in the Bahnhofsviertel.*

*The shaken victim stated a young woman tricked him into leaving a bar claiming she was too drunk to walk to the Hauptbahnhof alone. A man stopped them outside.*

*"When the victim kept walking, the man pulled out a knife. The victim was then knocked to the ground. The woman took his wallet. The robber then kicked the victim several times before running off." A Polizei officer said.*

*The suspects are a white female about 1.6 meters tall with blonde hair and a dark-skinned black male with shoulder length dreadlocks. The gang has an uncanny knack for picking victims with large amounts of cash.*

*Investigators believe they use prostitutes to lure victims away from well-lit areas. Visitors and residents are urged to travel in pairs and not flash money in clubs or bars.*

*The Polizei have increased patrols, especially on weekends.*

Lars folds the *Tagblatt* and answers his desk phone.

"Guten Morgen Herr Schollner."

"Guten Morgen Lars, your friend Nigel Trotter has three matches in Interpol's facial recognition system."

"Three? Do you have names?"

"Yes. They are…Nigel Trotter, Marcus Stoebel, and Franc Langenbrunner."

"Stoebel **and** Langenbrunner?" Lars blurts out.

"Yes, and all of them have a German class B license."

His pulse racing Lars furiously thumbs through his case file notes.

"Are you still there?" Schollner says.

"All three of those names are case workers on Doctor Kolb's patient list."

"I saw that. Either you have an identity thief or a spook."

"I agree-this case might crack wide open. Can you send me that information? Thank you, my friend, this is a great way to start a day."

---

Thirty minutes later Lars stares wide-eyed at copies of three German driver licenses.

"He's right they're identical! But who are the other two?"

His phone rings again.

"Detective Lars Kubach."

"Detective Kubach this is Jordan Forrest from *London University* Records. I'm calling in response to your email concerning Nigel Trotter. How may I assist you?"

"I'm conducting an investigation and I discovered he currently works here in Frankfurt."

"Are you sure it's him?"

Lars feels a knot tighten in his stomach.

"Yes…I…talked with him."

"Interesting, I did a search as you requested. According to our records he graduated in 1979 and I'm sorry to say but he has been deceased since two thousand seven."

Holding the phone from his ear Lars silently stares at his ticking office wall clock.

"Sir?"

"Detective, are you still there?"

# CHAPTER THIRTY-FIVE

**WEDNESDAY AFTERNOON:**

"ALEC LANDIS HERE. HOW MAY I help you Herr Kubach?"
His phone on speaker on his passenger seat Lars parallel parks across the street from the *Klaus Moritz Ubergangszentrum*.

"I'm calling about a former counselor named Franc Langenbrunner. How long did he work for the *Mannheim mental health clinic*?"

"He left here after nine months for a new position. In fact, I was his replacement."

"Do you know if he worked with a Doctor Victor Kolb?"

"I'm not certain about that sir."

"Did he say anything about his new position?"

"No sir, not to me. I only met him once."

"Does your clinic have his personnel file?"

"No sir it was deleted, we only keep them for ninety days."

"Thank you for your time, Herr Landis."

⁜

Frau Attiger pours coffee in two Styrofoam cups.

"How may I help you Herr Kubach?"

"I have more questions if you don't mind."

"Sure, the youth are on a field trip I get a rare break." She laughs guardedly.

"Inside this folder is a list of names and pictures I would like you to look over."

"Are they in some sort of trouble?"

"A thievery ring may be using them to commit crimes."

"Oh my, really?" Frau Attiger's face turns pale.

"Yes, it's a new wave of criminal activity, using children and troubled young adults as distractions for pickpockets and sometimes robbery."

"My what a horrible thing."

"I agree but I can't say more due to the investigation's sensitive nature."

He confirms his phony cover story with a fake frown.

"The faces are unfamiliar, but I keep records in my file cabinet, let me get them."

Back turned, Frau Attiger flips through a top drawer packed with labeled folders.

"They're not in here, but I have more records in the bottom drawer."

The long-necked fan is again useless, Lars wipes his sweat beaded forehead from the humidity and hot coffee.

He turns his eyes, avoiding staring at her ample rear bent over an open drawer.

"Here they are, I'm planning on digitizing them at some point."

She traces her finger down columns of penciled names in the curled yellow pages of a spiral bound ledger.

Inhaling a hint of perfume Lars leans over the desk examining it with her.

"I'm sorry detective but those names are not in here either."

"Was Nigel Trotter here today?"

"Yes, but he left early. And he is on vacation until next Friday."

*How convenient*

"Does he keep counseling records?"

"I'm sure he does, but they would be confidential."

"I know, but I just need to see if he counseled these individuals. I promise not to examine or divulge any personal information."

"Okay," she sighs, giving in to his imploring look, "but only for a few minutes. Follow me."

"He's been secretly smoking in here."

Pointing to a half-filled ashtray, Frau Attiger fans away the stale smell.

Lars thumbs through a stack of folders on Nigel's desk, pulling out a manila folder marked CASES.

"Wait, what's this?"

He hurriedly waves her over.

Her eyes widen as she slowly reads a document.

"That's one of the names you asked about. How did you know it would be here?"

"I had a hunch."

She stands by as he spreads out more pages.

"These are parental consent forms signed by the parents of Gunnar Weiss, Herman Renke, and Petr Nowak, allowing them to be counseled here."

"They are but that's not my signature."

"You never authorized these?"

"No, most of our referrals are from Catholic or other social services."

"The Saint Timothy Krankenhaus doesn't refer former patients here?"

"No sir we have no contract with them."

"And you never saw any of them or their parents?"

"I am here every day. I've never seen them. I do final interviews before approving counseling by Nigel."

"His notes state he counseled them here."

"But when?"

"Perhaps after hours, did he have keys?"

Her hands cover her mouth.

"Yes, oh my god, he's been lying to me, but why would he do this?"

"I can't say for sure just yet."

"Wait, are you hiding something? Is Nigel under some investigation?"

"Yes," Lars sighs, his eyes meet hers, "and I'm building my case. I need copies of those forms."

"Legally I can't allow it, but since he lied to me go ahead. If I do, wont it compromise your case since they are confidential?"

Lars looks around the office, his voice lowers.

"I'll take care of that but I need your cooperation for one other thing."

---

## LATE AFTERNOON: POLIZEI FORENSICS LAB

The well-dressed man appears twice in the grainy black and white video-entering and leaving forty-five minutes apart.

Jorge Stielhausner pauses the image and looks up at Lars.

"Where is this from?"

"It's the Ying's China Palace surveillance tape, I convinced the owner I needed to view it."

"And you want us to enhance it?"

"Yes, hopefully enough to identify his face."

"It's not the best but we'll see what we can do. I'll have my assistant run the face through our identity bank. Just give us a few days."

---

## WEDNESDAY EVENING

"Herr Kubach based on our initial counseling your father passed away when you were eight years old, and your mother and brother passed within the last year. I sense your recent actions are a result of not fully coming to terms with these losses. You also stated your ex-wife's remarriage brought up repressed memories of your divorce. I believe this may be a potential factor as well."

Doctor Bruno Klimowitz looks up from his notes. He lowers his glasses, peering over them at Lars.

"These factors combined with your prescreen questionnaire indicate your stress level is abnormally elevated."

"What do you recommend?"

"You were a semipro boxer and a regular jogger?"

"Yes, but lately I have gotten away from both."

"Returning to some physical activity is important. I suggest doing so as an alternative to stopping for a drink. Do you have other interests?"

"I collect Volks music."

"Create a playlist of favorite songs or just relax to it. Start with little things that you can control. But I also see you need to unburden yourself. Do you have people you feel comfortable talking with?"

*Frau Geiger... Oom?*

Thinking of them Lars nods.

"Ok good. I think continued counseling will help. We will forego any drug therapy for now. I will schedule you for a follow up appointment in a month. During that time, I want you to make a self-action plan for us to go over."

‧‧◆◆◆◆‧‧

## LATE EVENING: BAHNHOFSVIERTEL RED LIGHT DISTRICT

*"Go on get out!"*

Lars slams his brakes for a changing traffic signal.

His eyes wander to *DIVAS* flashing neon sign-and two men-the first, lanky with dreadlocks, faded jeans and a loose jacket, the other sporting neat cornrows.

They both give the Saab darting suspicious glances.

*"It's them."*

Timing the changing light, Lars zips through the intersection with his cell phone pressed to his ear.

"Feldwebel Schoepke speaking."

"Helmut, this is detective Kubach I may have a lead on the African gang."

"Really?" Schoepke's voice drops. "I'm under pressure about this, anything will help. What do you have?"

"I spotted two suspects matching their descriptions loitering by the black hole. I have a way to catch them."

"I'm open to suggestions, drop in my office."

<hr>

## THURSDAY TWO A.M. CLUB BACCHUS

The young man shifts his stool for a better view of the bar. Gripping an ice cube filled glass of Fanta his wide eyes nervously scan the soft lit main floor.

Scattered knots of men chat over drinks, others play team cricket on an LED dartboard.

Two men gently slow dance to background strains from Elton John's *Daniel*.

Two women, their faces almost touching, take matching straw sips from an oversized glass goblet.

A hand gently pats his shoulder.

"Is this your first visit?"

He shudders, swiveling his stool he faces a ruggedly handsome man in a fine tailored suit.

"A little shy, I understand, I'm Teddy Van Halst the owner, your next drink is on me. If you need anything else let me know."

Van Halst pats his shoulder again; his other hand casually brushes the visitor's thigh.

<hr>

Finished vomiting in a urinal the young man splashes cold water on his flushed cheeks.

He checks his bloodshot eyes in the bathroom mirror.

He opens his trembling palm showing two white pills, he takes a slow deep breath, tilts his head back and dry swallows them.

# CHAPTER THIRTY-SIX

**THURSDAY MORNING**

Hands clasped behind his back Lars paces a blood-soaked carpet- unable to recall a grislier murder in recent memory.

Covering his mouth Sergeant Detweiler narrates.

"The cleaning lady found the bodies. An ambulance took her away in state of shock."

His eyes tearing from the foul stench of body waste and coppery blood Lars crouches over the corpses.

Teddy Van Halst lays arms outstretched legs together his eyes gazing sightlessly at the drop ceiling.

A pocketknife buried to the handle protrudes from his throat.

He has so many stab-wounds-*forty, medical examiner Schmidt will later count*, that his entrails bulge out, reminding Lars of a grotesque extra-large American Jumbo.

The second face down body lays awkwardly sprawled across Teddy's chest.

A second blood smeared knife lies next his hand.

Lars looks up at Detweiler trying not to vomit.

"Looks like he slit his own wrists and bled out. Not a good day to be the coroner." Lars says.

Detweiler points to scattered piles of blood-stained money on Van Halst's desk.

"Robbery obviously was not a motive."

Lars gently turns the killer's head and gasps.

Detweiler stoops for a closer look; Herman Renke's unfocused eyes stare back at him.

"The kid from the protest?"

Lars grimly nods.

"Could it be from the teasing they gave him?"

"I think it's more than that."

Snapping on a pair of latex gloves, Lars pulls Renke's stiffening arm from his shirt sleeve exposing the armpit.

Still in a crouch Detweiler squints at two tiny black letters.

"A tattoo?"

"I've seen it before," Lars glances around the office, "I just wonder how he got back here."

"It might be on that security camera."

Detweiler points above the door.


## THURSDAY TEN P.M. CLUB BACCHUS

A flickered cigarette lighter shadows his face.

"We're closed." he says after a cough.

Subtly sizing up the barrel chested, bull necked bouncer, Lars flips open his wallet.

"Detective Lars Kubach Frankfurt police. I'm here to speak with the assistant manager."

The bouncer takes a long drag, he flicks the cigarette away, scattering glowing red embers on the sidewalk.

"He's waiting for you, there's no cover charge."

"Thanks."

Waiting for the ruddy cheeked Dirk Volmer to pour a glass of Dortmunder Union, Lars gazes at an impressive, array of liquor brands lined behind the bar counter.

"Thank you for opening to answer questions I know this can't be easy."

Dirk nervously massages his oiled and parted hairline.

"Certainly, better than a stuffy interview room."

"Did anyone see the killer?"

"I did. He sat in the seat next to you drinking cola."

His eyes shifting left, Lars stiffens and subtly slides his barstool.

"Teddy welcomed him. He greets every new face."

"He wasn't here before?"

"He came in near closing time, I've never seen him."

"What else did you notice?"

"He sat alone and didn't socialize."

"Did he exhibit any strange behavior?"

"If you count turning down date offers, then yes."

Lars cracks an uneasy smile.

"He did spend a long while in the bathroom. I think he threw up."

"Did he drink too much?"

"Not at all, just a Fanta, and a Red Bull."

"I reviewed the office security tape. Does mister van Halst normally admit visitors in the back?"

Dirk slams a shot of Jägermeister. He wipes his lip.

"Only if he knows them, that's where he locks up the nightly cash."

"No bouncer stayed behind?" Lars asks.

"No, he dismissed all of us early."

Biting his lip, Dirk stares at the bar counter.

After a long silence he looks up with moist eyes.

"Everyone is stunned, we are devastated by this."

++++++

## THE KAISER BISTRO: 1:45 A.M.

"Again, our top story, in Frankfurt, the respected owner of Club Bacchus was violently slain yesterday morning in what the Polizei are describing as a murder suicide."

The wall mounted tv screen switches to an earlier clip of Hauptmann Muller surrounded by reporters in front of Club Bacchus.

"Right now, there could be any number of reasons for this horrific crime, we urge everyone to avoid unwarranted speculation until our investigation is complete. We have no further comments."

Lars drains a last foamy swallow of Dortmunder Union.

"It's been on the news all day." The bartender says.

He wipes the counter and takes the empty glass.

"Last call, you want one more?"

"No thanks, I'm done." Lars mumbles.

He leaves forty Euros under a coaster, enough to cover five Dortmunder Unions.

--------------------◆◆◆◆◆--------------------

Whipping gusts from an approaching thunderstorm push against his back.

Ignoring aimless drug addicts and hookers he staggers past men clustered in front of bars and brothels.

CLUB APOLLYN's doorman shoves a flyer at him.

"Come in my friend, pretty girls waiting." He shouts over thumping dance music spilling out the open door.

Lars stumbles past him to the closed *Livorno Eis Café*.

His head spinning, he braces one arm on the graffiti painted exterior.

*"You are a Polizei, go check."*

*"She's going to think I did this!"*

*"Thank you for the wedding gift, Lars…"*

"Sir, are you okay?"

"I'm doing just fine." Lars slurs.

The man eyeing him takes a cautious step back.

"You should be careful those African robbers are still out here."

Shaking his head, the man watches him zigzag toward *Yildary's Kebab.*

A sweet-smelling haze of peppers, onions, and sizzling lamb wafts from the open sliding glass window.

A swarthy curly haired cook in a grease spattered apron looks up at Lars swaying outside.

"A shish kebab sounds good."

"Good for you to eat, soak up beer." The cook chirps in a high-pitched Middle East accent.

After several failed jabs to insert his ignition key, Lars rests his sweat beaded forehead on the steering wheel.

The images are back…*a* kaleidoscope of eyes…

*Brother Enoch's steely squint…*

*Victor Kolb's shifting gaze…*

*Nigel Trotter's penetrating pupils…*

*Oom's closed black almonds as she rides him in bed.*

*"You will see worse I promise."*

He shudders. More images…

*Frau Horst's half missing face…*

*Gabrielle Mecklenberg's grotesquely swollen purple bruised cheeks…*

*Ghastly images from Teddy Van Halst's ten-minute office slaughter video…*

His stomach gurgles, rising bile overfills his throat.

Heaving and coughing he yanks his door open.

Leaning out he vomits, the splashing foul-chunky liquid spreads like cake batter on the curb.

"Peter I'm sorry. I love you."

He flops in his seat shuddering and sobbing.

# CHAPTER THIRTY-SEVEN

## FRIDAY MORNING LARS KUBACH'S OFFICE

*"PEOPLE COMMIT MURDER FOR A variety of reasons, but certain high-profile killings follow a similar pattern known as the lone gunman syndrome. Support for this theory stems from the killers' remarkably identical actions before, during, and after the crime."*

*"The killers often have a history of antisocial behavior. Friends and family describe them as loners or trance like. Most received treatment for depression or other mental issues. Many were prescribed powerful psychosomatic drugs."*

Lars raises the volume on the You Tube video.

*"Survivors comment on the killers' blank expressions and robotic almost trancelike actions. Sirhan Sirhan who shot Robert Kennedy is a classic example of this disassociated state. I refer to it as specific amnesia."*

*"The killers that don't commit suicide after the murder claim no memories of events right before and during the crime as if their memory has been selectively erased."*

*"They tell of hearing disembodied voices or commands from television or radio. Examining doctors diagnose most of them with multiple personality disorders or schizophrenia."*

*"Media focus is always on the crime, not the underlying factors that caused them to do it, and once they are convicted or killed by their own*

*hand-the public never hears their side except for stories of their unstable behavior. But what makes them unstable?"*

*"It is well known that deep trance hypnosis can induce people to follow commands to bark like dogs or chirp like birds simply by use of trigger words or phrases. Could these sleepers as they are sometimes called be in a sort of semi-conscious state much like a sleepwalker who cannot remember what happened? Or is it something more sinister? Could they be mind-controlled killers for the illuminati?"*

Video paused; Lars chases two Motrin with a swallow of mineral water, he buries his pounding forehead in his palms.

His ringing phone makes the throbbing worse.

"Lars this latest murder could be a public relations nightmare, the gay community is going to explode if we don't do something."

"I'm on it sir. I scheduled a meeting with their leading activist and community leader."

<hr>

## A<small>FTERNOON</small>: N<small>EAR</small> G<small>OETHE</small> U<small>NIVERSITY</small> C<small>AMPUS</small>

Lars shakes hands with Jonathan Hobart, a flat stomached, muscular chested giant.

His skin-tight T shirt says BEING GAY MEANS I'M HAPPY.

"Good day detective Kubach I am the president of Resist, reaching equal status involves stopping tyranny."

"Pretty clever title."

Hobart waves at a shiny vinyl high backed chair.

"Won't you sit down?"

Lars scans framed pictures of famous gay personalities on the paneled wall behind Hobart's desk.

"Nice office you have."

"Shame I'm never in it, my work keeps me rather busy. I'd offer you coffee, but I am on a macrobiotic diet."

"I'm a boxer and a runner myself. I'll take a mineral water thank you."

"We both care about our body, that's good."

Winking subtly, Hobart hands Lars a bottle of Gerolsteiner from a mini refrigerator by his desk.

"It's obvious why I'm here Herr Hobart. What can you tell me about Mister Van Halst's murder?"

Hobart leans back in his swivel chair, gazing thoughtfully at the ceiling.

"Teddy was a longtime friend. He was well liked and enjoyed the unattached life. I think his death was religiously motivated."

His eyebrows rising Lars sits up straight.

"What makes you say that?"

"In the last few weeks protesters targeted my office and Teddy's club with graffiti."

"What type of graffiti?"

"Someone spray painted 'God is not mocked' on my window and his club."

"Could you describe the protesters?"

"I wasn't present, but Teddy said they were mostly women."

Lars takes a swallow of water and caps the bottle.

"Did you receive threats?"

"I always receive threats, mostly comments posted on our web site. I archive them to show the venomous hate we endure. They condemn us but their own King James was one of us."

Even Hobart's deep haughty laugh sounds muscular.

"So anyway, I called Teddy, and we agreed to meet any protest with counter protests intended to drive them off."

"I agree sir, but considering the killing's brutal nature, you should be careful. For any future protests call me immediately."

"No one gets in here—you see how I buzzed you in. We have cameras and I keep a full-time security guard. It's expensive but it's the price we pay to be different."

Hobart takes a long sip of water.

"I have a question for you detective."

"Go ahead sir."

"Were there markings on Teddy's body, a set of numbers by his groin perhaps?"

"How do you know that? No information has been publicly released."

Hobart flashes a curled enigmatic smile.

"Word travels fast in our community. Do you have a Bible handy?"

"We don't normally carry one." Lars says with a grin.

"Well, I do. I keep it in my desk."

He mockingly waves a well-worn black leather Bible, the cover and spine creased with spidery white cracks.

"This one was mailed to me by a Bible thumper a long time ago. I keep it for laughs."

Flipping to a bookmarked page, he sets the Bible on his desk facing Lars.

"Read Leviticus twenty thirteen."

Lars reads slowly out loud.

"If a man also lie with mankind, as he lieth with a woman, both of them have committed an abomination, they shall surely be put to death, their blood shall be upon them."

"That is their favorite verse to use against us. They even had the courtesy to highlight it to reveal my **sin**."

Hobart blinks repeatedly with smug haughtiness.

"Those numbers were on his body." Lars says softly.

"Doctor Schmidt told me. I'm guessing the other victims had similar numbers?" Hobart's eyebrows rise.

"Then they could be bible verses as well?"

"I don't know, no offense, but *you are* the detective."

Laughing again, Hobart rises from his chair, extending a bulging muscular forearm.

Lars stands up accepting his firm handshake.

"I assure you we will give this case priority."

"Don't do it for me, do it for Teddy."

## LATER: POLIZEI FORENSICS LAB

"We enhanced and colorized his face and matched him to a name."

Jorge Stielhausner drags Nigel Trotter's enlarged image next to a second picture.

Lars leans over his shoulder.

"An exact match?" he asks.

Stielhausner nods.

"The face on the left is Norman Ainsworth, a British citizen."

"Then who is the man in the video?" Rookie asks.

"It has to be Norman Ainsworth as well, because Nigel Trotter is dead."

The techs look sideways at each other, then Lars.

"Identity fraud?" rookie asks.

Lars nods.

"I need printouts of these images. I have further comparisons to make."

---

## SATURDAY ONE A.M. LARS KUBACH'S APARTMENT

*YOU AND YOUR KIND WILL ROT IN HELL!*

*Jahweh will never surrender to the demands of Jesus-phobes like you. 1 man 1 woman equals marriage.*

*2 men or 2 women equals a deserving death. You are a threat to society spreading diseases like aids and hepatitis and should be delivered unto Satan. …Faith defender*

The post in the RESIST website's comment section is two weeks old.

*"They even had the courtesy to highlight it to reveal my sin."*

With Hobart's sarcastic comment ringing in his ears Lars enters Leviticus 20-13 in an online King James Bible verse search tab and reads it again.

*If a man also lie with mankind, as he lieth with a woman, both of them have committed an abomination...*

His heart pounding, he enters the number from Doctor Klinsmann's left palm.

One of the twenty-two results catches his eye.

*Ezekiel 16-20 Moreover thou hast taken thy sons and thy daughters, whom thou hast borne unto me, and these hast thou sacrificed unto them to be devoured.*

His pulse racing, he enters the number from Frau Horst's body.

*Exodus 22-18 Thou shalt not suffer a witch to live.*

And finally; the numbers from Gabrielle Mecklenburg.

*Proverbs 7-27 Her house is the way to hell going down to the chambers of death.*

Stroking his chin Lars concentrates on the verse.

*"They even had the courtesy to highlight it to reveal my **sin**."*

"Wait a minute...seven two seven...Martyr for Jahweh. The stork's protest sign was Herman Renke's trigger!"

He glances at his LED alarm clock, ten minutes until Brother Enoch's broadcast.

Sweat beading on his forehead, he furiously finishes typing his laptop notes.

# CHAPTER THIRTY-EIGHT

## Two A.M.

"**W**ELCOME AGAIN LISTENERS, THIS IS the Jahweh's warrior's broadcast. Tonight, I will speak on the false prophecies of the Latter Rain Tabernacle."

"Jesus warned that in the last days that false prophets and false Christ's would show great signs and wonders to deceive many, if possible, even the very elect. We are witnessing the rise of false religions, and smooth-talking preachers using enticing words to spoil us through philosophy, deceit, and the traditions of men. Jahweh's word says that in these last days many shall depart from the faith and deny him, giving heed to seducing spirits and doctrines of devils bringing in damnable heresies. The latter rain tabernacle teaches one of those damnable heresies. Their leader preaches another Jesus, and another gospel. You say we should follow the commandments, obey the Sabbath and treat all things with respect and love. I say nonsense!"

Enoch takes a deep breath.

"The world is teeming in sin because you have neglected Jahweh's command to have dominion over the earth and to subdue it, and that won't happen by fasting or mourning or solemn vigils, **but with strength and power!**"

"You say Jesus is meek and humble, and we should turn the other cheek. You say sword and famine will not come…blah blah blah. The

Jesus I know will descend from heaven with a shout and a flaming sword, and as the first Enoch prophesied, he will come with **ten thousand saints!"**

**"We are those saints!** And our vengeance is soon. Your false prophecies have caused many to stumble. You evil men and seducers pretending to be apostles of Christ have turned his grace into commandments."

"I say we are not ignorant of Satan's devices and though you or an angel should preach another Jesus then you are cursed! Jahweh says we must **withdraw** and separate from disorderly brothers and those destitute of truth. And so now I, the second Enoch declare."

**"We withdraw** from you unruly vain talkers and deceivers who babble in strange tongues."

**"We withdraw** from your commandments and manmade doctrines."

**"We withdraw** from your corrupt minds of ignorance."

**"We withdraw** from your weak arguments and wasted time trying to achieve peace through silence and acceptance."

"You turned your backs on the truth and therefore we departed from you. Jahweh warned the prophet Jeremiah about false prophets saying I have not spoken to them, but they tell lies in my name. They use deceit and say God says this or God says that."

"But just as Jahweh loved Jacob and hated Esau so it is with us and you. And one day you will come to us on broken knees like Esau. And your latter rain shall never arrive. And soon the world shall see the punishment of your sins."

---

Brother Enoch slips off his headphones.

He turns to the young man with him in the homemade studio.

"Young brother by the power given to me, the second Enoch by almighty Jahweh I send you forth, go and prepare the way of the Lord."

# CHAPTER THIRTY-NINE

## SATURDAY MORNING: TEN A.M.

**B**ORNHEIM IS A CHEERY NEIGHBORHOOD of pubs, cafes, cider houses and restaurants.

On Saturdays it hosts an open-air farmer's market.

Inhaling mixed aromas, Lars strides past food stalls offering fresh fruits, vegetables, butchered meats, and various warm baked goods; his target is on a side street five minutes away.

---

Waiting for an answer to his knock, Lars reads a welcome sign in a glass case.

*The Latter Rain Tabernacle*
Pastor Werner Kruge
Service time: Sunday 10:00 A.M.
*Break up your fallow ground and seek the LORD till he come and rain righteousness upon you.* Hosea 10:12

---

"I'm Werner Kruge senior pastor. Come in please."

A middle-aged sandy haired man with a broad rosy cheeked smile greets Lars with a warm handshake.

He's dressed conservative-corduroy pants, a button-down long sleeve shirt.

His modest 'office' is remarkably plain; a desk, and a bookshelf stocked with well-worn Bible commentaries.

He notices Lars gazing at the bare stucco walls.

"If you're looking for the usual church trappings you won't find them here. We don't have paintings of Christ or fancy crosses. Jesus isn't on the cross anymore he's at the father's right hand waiting to bring us the latter rain. We are peace loving folk who live according to the early church doctrines. We don't wear suits and ties; we gather here to pray and fellowship."

Nodding respectfully Lars takes the chair Kruge offers.

His elbows propped on his desk, Kruge folds his hands under his chin.

"So how may I help you detective?"

"I'm here to ask questions about a recent schism in your church."

"Ahh yes, Brother Enoch. He was too radical for us, almost like the dominionists."

"I'm sorry I don't understand."

"The best way to describe it is as a Christian version of Sharia law. Dominionists teach the superiority of the Christian faith over other religions. They believe governments should rule by Biblical precepts."

"Brother Enoch held this belief?"

"To the point where he claimed that God raised him as the second Enoch to condemn the world. We…" Kruge spreads his arms, "are not here to condemn. As Jesus told the woman caught in adultery, neither do I condemn thee go and sin no more."

"What caused the divide?"

"He insisted that praying and fasting are not answers to the world's problems. To him sin is a cancer that must be dealt with and the only way to do so is to confront it with force if necessary. We of course don't teach such an unbiblical view."

"I listened to him last night. It sounds just like what you are saying."

"He *can* be rather convincing."

"Would you consider him prone to violence or anger?"

"We consider him one of the false prophets mentioned in Matthew twenty-four."

"Has he or any of his followers threatened you?"

"No sir but we don't worry, the Lord will protect us as he always has."

"I agree but I still think you should be careful he mentioned your church in his broadcast."

"We will sir. Is there anything else?"

"No sir I just thought you should know."

Kruge pushes out his chair, he warmly pats Lars on the shoulder.

"Thank you detective Kubach and you are welcome to join us anytime."

His back turned in the doorway Lars pauses.

"Is something the matter?" Kruge asks.

"Do you know any other members of his church?"

"Yes, one of his major backers was a man named Thorsten Keitel. He worked at *Deutschland Novelties and Souvenir Exports*."

Lars pulls out a notepad and a pen from his jacket.

"Thorsten Keitel? You're sure he worked there?"

"Well, I shouldn't say *worked* there, actually he's the owner."

Lars almost drops his pen.


## SATURDAY AFTERNOON

Founded in 2006, Deutschland Novelties and Souvenir Exports is an online store dedicated to selling all things uniquely German. We specialize in hard-to-find items along with an impressive array of cuckoo clocks, Bier steins, and traditional clothing. We ship locally and internationally. So, if you are looking for that rare collectible or just want to send a unique gift to a friend, we are the place to order from. Please allow 3 to 6 weeks for overseas shipments. Thank you in advance for your order.

Scrolling through the company homepage Lars puts Manfred Schollner on speaker.

"Someone named faith defender wrote the comment?" Schollner says.

"Yes, and one other thing, I did some research. Nigel Trotter is dead and a man named Norman Ainsworth is using his ID to commit identity fraud and also apparently posed as Langenbrunner and Marcus Stoebel. He is connected to the cult. I need to know who he really is."

"I'll search our database on him and this faith defender."

"Thank you, old friend the quicker the better."

# CHAPTER FORTY

## RED LIGHT DISTRICT: SUNDAY 1 A.M.

HIDDEN FROM THE MAIN STREETS leading away from the Hauptbahnhof, *"the black hole"* is where heroin addicts, crack smokers, and junkies gather to get high.

The narrow passage's other nickname, *Addicts Alley* is a pun on the Polizeipräsidium Adickesallee street address.

The Polizei tolerate it, dispatching occasional patrols when workers from the *Mary Magdalene Social Center* distribute clean needles and hygienic supplies.

From his unmarked car Sergeant Ulf Wetzel keeps a sleepy vigil on the wandering zombies, furtive drug transactions, and drunken knots of foreigners staggering between brothels and bars.

No one notices the curled body on a grated metal bench, until now...

Suddenly awake Wetzel straightens up.

---

Drunkenly swaying, Thaddeus Mitchell exits the *Innus Lauf Haus* clumsily zipping up his pants.

His orgiastic evening of peep shows, table dances, and prostitutes cost three hundred Euros.

He stumbles past mannequins lining *NYMPHOS* sex shop window and stops at *Domenici's Pizza.*

Holding a grease dripping pizza slice with one hand, Thaddeus pauses by the bench to wipe his mouth.

He stoops for a closer look and jerks back wrinkling his nose from the powerful wine stench.

The 'body' is a passed out drunk.

"Piece of shit." Thaddeus mutters and staggers away.

At the next corner, a pale skeletal hooker lifts her shirt exposing her breasts and sharply outlined ribcage.

Following her shifting eyes to the black hole, Thaddeus feels his pockets for his last fifty Euro note.

A lanky dark skinned dreadlocked man slowly follows them, nodding at a man with thick cornrows leaning on a poster covered concrete pillar across the street.

Watching them the whole time Sergeant Wetzel adjusts his earpiece.

"It's them." A crackling voice confirms.

———————— ·+·✦✦·+· ————————

Behind a dumpster with his pants at his ankles Thaddeus hears a metallic click.

"I'll stab you man don't look at me." A thick accented voice says. "Pull your pants up real slow."

"Wait, please don't hurt me."

"Shut the fuck up and empty your pockets."

"Ok ok."

Instantly sober Thaddeus slides up his pants.

"Give her your money!"

Still on her knees the hooker snatches his fifty Euro note.

"That's it?" The mugger hisses.

"I swear man that's all I have."

Her eyes widening, the hooker silently points to an approaching silhouette.

The mugger whirls around; instantly blinded by a piercing light, he shields his face with a raised arm.

"What the fuck?"

"Halt, Sie sind verhaftet!"

Keeping his flashlight trained on the mugger's face Sergeant Wetzel unholsters the pistol on his waist belt.

"You're under arrest!" he repeats, "Get down now!"

The dreadlocked mugger waves the switchblade in his right hand.

His twisted smile reveals a row of gold fillings.

"Look behind you pig."

Wetzel spins around.

Grinning wickedly the corn rowed man strides toward him smacking a metal pipe on his palm.

Wetzel's eyes dart between both muggers. Taking a defensive stance, he sweeps his pistol back and forth.

"Both of you stay where you are."

Corn row turns his head sharply; he suddenly drops the pipe and sprints from the alley.

A Polizei car roars past in a blur of flashing lights.

A second cruiser screeches to a stop, blocking the black hole entrance.

The doors fly open, two officers with guns drawn race up the alley.

Both hands gripping his pistol, Wetzel aims at the dreadlocked mugger.

"Drop the knife now!" he shouts.

Dreadlock drops the switchblade and raises his hands.

Minutes later Sergeant Schoepke stands over the facedown handcuffed mugger and the prostitute.

"Team two nabbed the other one, looks like we finally caught them." He says with a victorious grin.

"Their robbery spree is over." Wetzel sighs in relief.

They both glare sternly at Thaddeaus.

"You are very lucky." Wetzel says.

"Thank you, officers, thank you."

Head down to avoid their scolding frowns, an embarrassed Thaddeaus zips up his pants.

# CHAPTER FORTY-ONE

**MONDAY: BAHNHOFSVIERTEL STATION**

**ROBBERY GANG ROUNDED UP**

FRANKFURT – THE AFRICAN GANG members responsible for a terrifying two-month robbery spree were arrested over the weekend. Two Nigerian nationals are charged with robbery, assault, and pimping. Their female companion was released.

The duo committed numerous robberies in the Bahnhofsviertel, preying on tourists and visitors. It's estimated they netted over two thousand Euros by posing as beggars, selling fake merchandise, and recruiting drug addicted prostitutes as bait.

"They were very clever to elude us by moving around. But early last week we received a tip they were using an alley as a setup area. We were fortunate enough to catch them in the act. We are glad to put this behind us." A Polizei spokesperson said.

Grinning widely, Lars folds the Frankfurter Allegemeine.

His coffee mug is at his lips when his mobile rings.

"Detective Kubach."

"Ah good to catch you, this is Doctor Schmidt. I am calling about Herman Renke."

"Go on."

"He ingested about twenty-five hundred milligrams of Halodan."

"The normal dose is five hundred, correct?"

"Yes, one tablet every eight hours."

"So, if he took five at once what would happen?"

"He would have become violently sick. The tablets were most likely taken over a two or three-hour period."

"If he took them that way, what would the effects be?"

"It would have put him in an agitated trance like state."

"Enough to commit a violent murder suicide?"

"It's a possibility, and by the way my apologies for leaking information without your approval, but Johnny is a good friend of mine."

"I'm glad you did it may help crack the case. Thank you, Herr Schmidt."

His phone rings again; sighing he lowers his cup a second time.

"Detective Kubach."

"Guten Morgen my friend. What I discovered about Norman Ainsworth might surprise you."

"What is it, Herr Schollner?"

"Scotland Yard has an open case file on his involvement in a London insurance scam."

"That might explain Nigel Trotter's designer clothes and newer model van."

Schollner chuckles.

"And-the slew of fake identities-facing potential jail time he cooperated with investigators and received five years' probation and a fine."

"Let me guess, he ratted on his partners."

"Exactly."

"Is there a record?"

"Just a vague charge of financial irregularities."

"So why is there still an open file?"

"Scotland Yard recently requested Interpol to issue a blue notice on him. It came to our office about two months ago. I found out during my search. I'll sneak a copy to your email."

"I owe you lunch my friend thank you."

His phone buzzes again, this time it's a text alert.

*In my office immediately.*

"Damn it!"

He gulps the now lukewarm coffee and grabs his keys.

<hr/>

Muller's arms are folded on his desk. Sergeant Schoepke stands beside him, arms crossed like a sentinel.

They both have faint grins.

"Sergeant Schoepke tells me you helped catch the African gang."

"Yes sir."

"Pretend to be a drunk and wear a microphone, pretty clever." Muller says.

"It's an old trick from my street days."

Sergeant Schoepke offers a handshake.

"Thank you, detective Kubach."

Muller clears his throat.

"Now on to the next matter, the latest killing has the entire city on edge. The mayor has set a Friday deadline to prove your case, or it will be handed to the BKA. Shurtzmann wants a complete report by Wednesday morning."

"I have everything in my office. I can give it to you now."

"Save it for then." Muller says with a dismissive wave. "There is something else we need to discuss."

On Muller's nod Schoepke leaves the room, patting Lars on the shoulder on his way out.

"Thank you again detective Kubach."

"At least your case is solved." Lars whispers.

<hr/>

Hands on his hips, Muller paces behind his desk.

"Your friend is still being stubborn. She refuses to cooperate unless she can meet with you."

"And?"

"I'll have her released if you can persuade her to our demands."

"And they are?"

Muller stops and turns.

"Lock the door."

———————— +·+·+·+·+·+ ————————

## Monday evening

Holding hands Lars and Oom stroll through the Palmengarten.

He scans the rolling dark clouds gathering in the distance.

"Finally, a break from the heat."

"Yes, my first freedom in a week. Maybe rain later. You can smell in the air."

"Tell me the truth. You were going to blackmail them?"

"Not me, the girl said Polizei officers make sex film of her at party."

Lars looks at her with raised eyebrows.

"Hauptmann Muller never mentioned a sex film. Was she freelancing?"

"What is freelancing?"

"Did she do this on her own?"

"No, a man come in pay for her to go with him."

"Did he say what for?"

"They never say what for, I don't ask."

"Did you know he was a Polizei officer?"

"Yes, and when they don't pay her, I keep his credit card deposit."

"A bar fine? You know that's not allowed."

"Not allowed, but I lose many customers because of murder and gang robbers."

"Was the girl raped?"

"No, but she make threat to tell news about secret book."

"I remember the Tagblatt article, does she have your black book?"

"No, she lied to Polizei. She tell them I plan to sell it to Tagblatt and expose them. Polizei arrest me for blackmail but I not make any threat."

They stop at the park fountain; she releases his hand.

"Polizei close my business, hold all my workers on immigration charges and want to fine me fifty thousand Euros. I don't have that."

"Hauptmann Muller will drop the charges and clear you of all fines if you return the officer's credit card deposit and publicly admit the black book is a rumor."

"What about my workers?"

"I don't think I can stop any deportations."

Sighing, Oom shakes her head.

"So now I lose more money. I don't like this."

Side by side they silently watch the spraying fountain.

Lars gently slides his arm around her shoulders.

"Ok, ok I do it." she finally says.

"Great, I will tell Muller right away."

Lars wraps his arms around her pulling her close.

"I looked up Werner Musselman. You married an expat?"

"He was Frau M's friend. They make fake resident permit for girls to come to Germany."

"Then they *were* running a mail order bride website?"

"Yes, he posts bar girls pictures online, she finds men to marry them."

"Why didn't she hire legal workers?"

"Because too much paperwork and that way she only pays city fees for registered workers."

"Is this site still on the internet?"

"No, she take it down when talk with police."

"What about the men?"

"Some stay married some take payment and get divorce."

"Why wasn't she jailed?"

"You ask many questions. When arrested, she agreed to remove famous people names from book, so police won't charge her."

"A plea deal. They wanted you to do the same thing."

"Yes, the girl told police that police president visits for massages and sex."

"Polizeipräsident Shurtzmann?"

Oom laughs at his harsh whisper and wide eyes.

"He visits secretly. I only give him a real massage one time."

"So that's the real reason for the raid. They were worried about another secret book."

Oom laughs.

"They waste their time. I keep it but only for payment records, no names just card numbers."

Grinning broadly Lars grips her shoulders, his hands inch down her back to her waist.

Noses touching, they stare into each other's eyes.

"I'm sorry I got mad at you." he says.

"I sorry too, maybe I think about quitting business."

She pushes away his kiss attempt.

"You still can't fall in love with me."

"What do you mean?"

Head down, she shuffles her feet.

"I was a bar girl too. I dance in many Bangkok clubs. I don't know if I can ever fall in love."

# CHAPTER FORTY-TWO

### TUESDAY: BAHNHOFSVIERTEL POLIZEI STATION

T APPING HIS FEET TO A German singer's version of Neil Diamond's Sweet Caroline, Lars answers his office phone.

"May I speak with detective Lars Kubach?"

He lowers the radio volume.

"Speaking."

"Herr Kubach this is Gertrude Neubauer."

"Ahh Frau Neubauer, how may I help you?"

"I'm calling from work. Can we meet somewhere privately over lunch perhaps?"

"Name the place."

* ◆◆◆◆◆ *

A short walk from Bockenheim's Saint Jacob's church, *Gerhardt's Restaurant* serves traditional German cuisine; it claims to have the best steaks in Frankfurt.

The shiny pine floor, solid oak tables, frilled white tablecloths, and crystal chandeliers all support the exclusive restaurant's consistent rave reviews from fine dining blogs and culinary magazines.

A busy wait staff in royal blue vests and starched ivory frilled shirts covers the packed dining room.

Seated by the large plate glass window, Lars sips an overpriced Asbach Uralt and Coke, watching a silver BMW E93 convertible glide into a parking space across the street.

Gertrude closes the hard top with her key fob, and crosses the street adjusting a Gucci purse slung over her cream-colored blazer.

· · · · · · · ·

Up close she looks elegant; late-forties, salon styled auburn hair, and perfectly applied makeup.

Lars slides out her chair.

"You sounded troubled on the phone."

"I know my husband wishes to protect our family name, but I need to set the record straight."

Lars raises his eyebrows.

"What do you mean?"

Her ocean blue eyes stare at the floor, she sighs heavily.

"He doesn't know I'm meeting you and if you don't mind-"

"I promise our conversation will never leave this restaurant."

"Ever since the killing, my coworkers have avoided me like the plague. I took stress leave, but I can't handle this anymore."

"There's something else isn't there?"

"Yes, I'm afraid we were not entirely truthful with you. But we didn't know what to say being in shock and all."

"Here comes our waiter. Let's order first."

The sandy haired waiter takes back their three-page menu cards and verifies their orders, a Caesar salad, and a bowl of potato soup for Gertrude and a pan seared flank steak for Lars.

"And two glasses of Riesling please." Gertrude adds as he walks away.

She takes a drink of Rosbacher mineral water from a crystal encrusted glass, dabbing her lips with a tri-folded cloth napkin.

"I've read the recent headlines about the murders."

"I've been working diligently on them."

Gertrude looks him in the eye.

"They're connected, aren't they?"

Lips pursed; Lars subtly nods.

"In a number of ways."

"I'm not sure if it will help but Hans had an incident during his senior year. We received an emergency call from the *Wurzburg Krankenhaus*. The Polizei caught him defacing an adult store window."

Imagining a spray-painted red x, Lars shifts in his seat.

"To make a long story short their report said he was babbling and incoherent."

"Was this the first incident?"

"No, he had been seeing a counselor for a few months prior. It was the stress he told us. My husband and I drove all the way to Wurzburg the next morning."

Their heads turn to the waiter balancing a tray with a raised arm.

Smiling politely, he sets down their orders, bows slightly, and leaves for another table.

Gertrude and Lars clink their raised wine glasses and take matching sips.

Lars slices his steak and brings a forkful to his mouth.

"Please continue." he says.

"When we arrived, the counselor was waiting."

"What was his name?"

"If I recall, his last name was Stoebel."

"Marcus Stoebel?"

"Yes, that's it. Do you know him?"

"Not as well as I would like."

"Well anyway I thought it strange that he had a German name but spoke with a British accent."

*It's him, Norman Ainsworth!*

"He said the bizarre behavior would continue without treatment. Of course," she takes another sip, "I didn't believe him."

"What did he recommend?" Lars asks, wary of the answer he knows is coming.

"He recommended Hans see a specialist in Frankfurt for outpatient treatment."

"May I ask the specialist's name?"

"Doctor Victor Kolb."

Lars drops his fork; it clatters on the plate; curious faces glance and turn quickly away.

"Is something the matter?"

"No excuse me. Please go on."

"When Hans was discharged, we pleaded with him to finish his last two semesters, but he refused."

"Did he provide a reason?"

Gertrude chases a forkful of salad with a sip of wine.

"Do you remember I said he became troublesome?"

"I recall that yes."

"As you know we are Catholic, but Hans claimed the Catholic Church is mystery Babylon-whatever that means."

"Did he ever say if his new church was helping him?"

"No, he was secretive about it, and we didn't ask. I wish we would have."

"Was he taking any medicine?"

Head down, Gertrude twirls a romaine leaf in a cup of vinegar; she looks up with teary eyelashes.

"Yes, and that's why I finally decided to contact you. I read about Halodan being an experimental drug and when you called my husband..." she clears her throat, "Well it brought back unpleasant memories."

"Did doctor Kolb prescribe it?"

"Not initially, he recommended it just before Hans was released. We thought it would help."

"Did his behavior change?"

"I didn't notice. But I'm just tired of our son being portrayed as some sick murderer. My husband is drinking heavily and it's wearing on our marriage. Do you think the drug may have driven our son to kill?"

His shifting eyes scan the nearby tables, he leans close, his voice lowered.

"Frau Neubauer, I know they are confidential, but could you get me copies of your son's treatment records."

"I have them somewhere at home yes."

He slides a card in her palm.

"Thank you, here is my contact information. I will also email you two pictures that I want you to identify."

"Please keep this between us Lars."

"Of course. There's one last thing. Do you recall if mister Stoebel was a smoker?"

"Yes, he and my husband went outside together."

---

The call comes with Lars stopped at a traffic light.

"Lars, it's Manfred. I traced the threatening comment, it was sent by a Thorsten Keitel. I saved you time and looked him up."

"Is he the same Thorsten Keitel who owns an export business?"

"Yes…How did you know?"

"His office is downtown. I plan to visit him anyway, now I have a valid reason."

# CHAPTER FORTY-THREE

S IPPING A DORTMUNDER UNION LARS reads a printed copy from the *Wurzburg Krankenhaus Mental Hygiene Dept.*

*The patient, a 22-year-old German male has been under my counseling and advisement since 2-15-08. Patient displays brief bouts of reality dissociation between longer periods of lucidity. Patient exhibits antisocial behavior and experiences auditory hallucinations of a paranoid nature. In meeting with parents, I advised them he is unlikely to improve without treatment as condition shows signs of being progressive. Parents' consent to have him admitted on outpatient basis and have read and understand all risks and responsibilities regarding treatment. As per parent's request patient's name is withheld. Admissions form signed by parents in my presence on this day 6-18-08.*

"Signed by Marcus Stoebel."

Lars saves the document and opens Frau Neubauer's second scan from the Saint Timothy Krankenhaus.

*This is to certify that Hans Neubauer, 22 years old has been authorized for outpatient treatment of acute paranoia effective 6/20/08. Parents have read and understood that treatment regimen includes possible use of experimental drug therapy and relinquish any rights to pursue legal action and hold myself and Saint Timothy Krankenhaus responsible for potential damages resulting from such treatment. Parents also understand that rescinding outpatient status is contingent upon my determination that it is safe to do so.*

"Signed by Doctor Victor Kolb. So, Hans Neubauer was the redacted name on his patient list. Now the connection is too obvious."

His beer finished; he opens Gertrude's email reply.

*Herr Kubach:*

*The pictures you sent are our son's social worker Marcus Stoebel. Thank you for your help during our most difficult times. Good luck with your investigation.*

"She identified both pictures of Norman Ainsworth. Good luck indeed!" Lars says out loud.

He glances at his clock radio; he has five minutes to pee and get another beer.

## 2 A.M. SHORTWAVE BROADCAST

"The word of Jahweh says a false witness shall be punished and he that speaks lies shall perish."

"Jesus pronounced seven woes upon the scribes and Pharisees. And now I as his messenger pronounce seven woes on today's scribes and Pharisees."

"**Woe** unto you greedy televangelists! You deceive the poor to increase your riches. Your gold and silver is cankered and their rust is a witness against you. Your riches will be corrupted, and your garments will be moth eaten."

"**Woe** unto you false teachers! You shall not prosper, and all your flocks shall be scattered. Your congregation of hypocrites shall be desolate, and fire shall consume your tabernacles of bribery."

"**Woe** unto you foolish prophets! You follow your own spirit and have seen nothing! Your lips speak lies, your tongues mutter perverse things. You violate the law and profane the holy things."

"**Woe** unto you lukewarm pastors! You live in pleasure and lack nothing. The cares of this world have choked you and made you unfruitful. Therefore, Jahweh will spit you out of his mouth."

"**Woe** unto you scholars who corrupt the word of Jahweh! The wind shall eat you up, you will go into captivity, and you shall be ashamed and confounded for your wickedness."

"**Woe** unto you priests who cause the people to error by telling lies in Jahweh's name when he has not spoken. You cater to the will of the people who say prophesy unto us smooth things and prophesy deceits."

"**Woe** unto you shepherds that feed yourselves and not the flocks! You destroy and scatter the sheep and lead them astray. And just as the angel in revelation said one woe is past behold there cometh two more woes."

"Jahweh will punish all of you, his hand shall be upon your vanity and lies and you will not be assembled with his people at the judgment seat and they that follow you shall meet the same fate! Despite your pleas and protests he will command you depart from me I never knew you and shall cast you into the lake of fire and **brimstone**!"

"Therefore, you shepherds, hear the word of Jahweh. Behold, I am against you, and I will require my flock at your hand, and *you* shall fall by the sword."

"The prophet Jeremiah wrote cursed are they that keep their sword from blood. If we keep our sword from blood, we are the cursed ones."

"And now I close with a call to all warriors prepared to fight evil. All things are purged with blood and without bloodshed there is no forgiveness of sin. Behold the battle cry is in the land, Jahweh orders us to heed the trumpet and punish the evil doers."

"Elijah said, take Baal's prophets and let none of them escape. Let us to do the Lord's work and slay them at the brook of Kishon **here and now!**

"**A sword is upon the liars**! And the punishment of the prophet shall be the same for them that listen to him. Three shepherds will I cut off in one month, howl ye shepherds and cry for the days of your slaughter for we shall smite the shepherd and the sheep shall be scattered!"

The young man known as Elijah turns the radio off.

Panting, his cheeks flushing, he stares wide eyed at the breathing walls closing in on him.

"Are you ok?" his roommate asks from his bunk.

"I'm good just feeling nervous."

"You are doing the right thing. Jahweh will guide you."

"I know Gunnar, I know."

# CHAPTER FORTY-FOUR

O N HOLD, WITH THE RECEIVER pressed to his ear, Lars shoots glances at his wall clock ticking toward ten a.m.

He twists a pen between his free fingers.

"Come on, come on." he says under his breath.

Five clock glances later, the *Wurzburg Krankenhaus*, record custodian is back on the line.

"Herr Kubach, mister Stoebel worked here for less than a year, and left for another position. I'm sorry but we have no further information, we delete records after six months if someone quits."

"Then he did quit?"

"Yes, is there anything else I may help you with?"

"No thank you, Frau Rorbach."

Lars hangs up and clicks a newly arrived email.

"From Alec Landis?"

*I probably shouldn't do this, but I found some information on Franc Langenbrunner.*

------------ ◦◦◦◦◦◦ ------------

## POLIZEIPRÄSIDENT SHURTZMANN'S OFFICE

"You look tired detective. Close the door."

Shurtzmann waves Lars to a chair facing his desk.

"My apologies sir I was up late preparing my report."

Ignoring Hauptmann Muller's skeptical frown Lars hands Shurtzmann a stuffed manila folder.

The background fish tank hums quietly as Shurtzmann slowly flips through the pages.

"So let me get this straight, a fake counselor with multiple aliases refers patients to a fake doctor who administers an experimental drug, then, after listening to a preacher rant and rave single young men go out and kill?"

"It's all there, sir."

Shurtzmann and Muller share doubtful sideways glances.

"Explain to us how this works." Muller says.

"Of course, it's never been proven but there are theories about people known as Manchurian candidates. A skilled therapist can create an urge or desire to kill on demand by a subject."

Muller leans back in his chair staring silently at the office ceiling.

"You're expecting us to believe these guys were what- programmed killers for some cult?" He finally says.

"I believe Jahweh's warriors are that cult. The numbers on each victim's autopsy photos are bible verses related to what would be considered their sins. And…" Lars takes a breath, "Brother Enoch's arrival in Frankfurt coincides with everything in my report."

"I'm still unclear on this, what would be the motive?" Shurtzmann says.

"Some radical Christian branches are rabidly against abortion, homosexuality and witchcraft."

"Such fringe groups are vocal about these issues, but I have a hard time believing they would risk killing, knowing they would likely be caught."

"Please fill in just how this would happen." Muller curtly interrupts.

"A person can be induced to kill as I said. Known as a sleeper they are activated by trigger words or repeated verbal messages combined with drug use."

Shurtzmann folds his arms across his chest.

"This sounds too bizarre. I'm having trouble believing in sleepwalking killers and I'm sure the mayor will too."

"As you can see sir, I have enough evidence."

"Ok, let's go over it. Start with Nigel Trotter. What is his role in all this?"

Shurtzmann looks up expectantly at Lars.

"In his role as counselor he referred Gunnar Weiss, Herman Renke, Petr Nowak, and Detlef Bergmeyer to Doctor Kolb. His employer at the Klaus Moritz Übergangszentrum was unaware he used phony documents to release the first three from the Saint Timothy Krankenhaus to the shelter. None of them were ever there."

"Ok, but my next question is, who are the other two counselors?"

"I received an email this morning from the Mannheim clinic of Mental Health. The document shows Franc Langrenbrunner counseled Matthias Hinkel and referred him to Doctor Kolb in Frankfurt."

Shurtzmann flips through the report.

"Continue detective." He says without looking up.

"Hans Neubauer was referred to Doctor Kolb by Marcus Stoebel in Wurzburg."

"You state here," Muller flips to a page, "that Nigel Trotter is actually dead, and Norman Ainsworth stole his identity. Tell me more."

Lars clears his throat.

"I determined that Norman Ainsworth obtained Nigel Trotter's ID and used it to create a series of aliases."

"You mean Langenbrunner and Stoebel?"

"Yes, and since all their faces are identical, I ran them through the Central register of driving licenses. Only Nigel Trotter is officially in the system. There are no records of the other two taking the theoretical or practical tests. I also searched numerous potential driving schools and found no records either. Yet all three counselors had German driver licenses issued within the last two years."

Shurtzmann flips through more pages.

"The Interpol blue notice states this Ainsworth character defaulted on paying insurance fraud penalties. Seems he's been committing fraud for some time."

"Yes sir, that explains his movements from place to place under different names. Scotland Yard might want to know about his latest gig as a youth counselor."

"We should not involve them yet." Shurtzmann says.

Lars looks at Shurtzmann with arching eyebrows.

"Why not?"

"There is enough media scrutiny as it is. And there are too many tenuous connections between these persons."

"Sir, I have carefully outlined the relations between Norman Ainsworth, Doctor Victor Kolb, and Brother Enoch."

"Then tell me about Doctor Kolb's connection."

"Four of his patients committed murder and two others including my brother committed suicide."

Lars looks down for a silent moment, then sighs.

"To be fair, I'm not ruling out the possibility that the medicine he prescribed them is a factor."

"You were told Halodan is off limits."

Lars glares sideways at Muller's interruption.

"Are we on that again sir?"

"I know your brother's loss makes it personal, but Doctor Kolb did not kill anyone. Your proof of his involvement is border line."

"But his patients did! He is connected sir, no matter what you say. He should be brought in for questioning."

"All right, all right," Shurtzmann waves his arms. "Stop it both of you."

He leans forward his fingers laced under his chin.

"Detective, it seems Norman Ainsworth and Doctor Kolb *are* connected, but Brother Enoch just sounds like a kook."

"It's not in my report, but Nigel Trotter aka Norman Ainsworth is a deacon in Brother Enoch's church. He admitted that Petr Nowak spent time there. He was vague about Nowak's job searches or his current whereabouts."

"Are you saying this Nowak is dangerous?"

"I don't have proof, just a hunch. I tried contacting his parents, but the number is not in service."

Shurtzmann's skeptical eyes shift to Mueller.

"Ok, now tell me about this website comment."

"It was sent by a man named Thorsten Keitel two weeks before Teddy Van Halst's murder. During my interview he affirmed supporting Brother Enoch but claims he cut ties when Enoch defaulted on a loan to start his broadcast."

"To me it seems like venting from a person with a lot of misguided hate. I think he's nothing more than a religious zealot. No need to go further."

"But there is sir. He became visibly agitated when I asked about his employee, Marianna Obermayer. She was present at the last two protests and is an active cult member. Keitel supported Brother Enoch and he might still be-using Frau Obermayer as a money launderer."

"I get it, but you haven't provided a consistent narrative. Is it botched therapy? Prescription drugs? A weird cult ritual? Right now, we are forced to create individual motives rather than a group effort."

"I agree," Muller interrupts, "Despite Ainsworth's fraud do you *have* proof other than speculation?"

Lars throws up his hands.

"What will it take, a massacre? While you protect a pharmaceutical company's reputation, I wish to prevent the next killing!"

He pushes his chair, stomps off and slams the door.

Muller bolts up after him.

"He was up late all right-probably drinking. I'll order him back in."

Shurtzmann holds up a restraining palm.

"Let him go."

"Sir he just…"

"Never mind."

Shurtzmann paces silently, hands on his hips.

"Has the Sauna issue been dealt with?"

"Yes, I released Oom. I thought it might relieve some of his stress."

"We're not here about Detective Kubach's stress. The mayor wants this out of the media, and I plan to do so."

"How sir?"

"Your detective has left me no choice. I'm requesting the BKA take over."

He locks eyes with Mueller.

"You are not to tell him nothing."

# CHAPTER FORTY-FIVE

"THIS IS MY FIRST TIME here."

The visitor shakes the smiling aged usher's hand and follows him to a shiny varnished wood bench.

Flipping through a hardcover hymnal book, he sneaks glances at the eager waiting faces.

Wearing a tan cloth tunic and cradling a metal urn, Brother Enoch struts to the pulpit.

He sets the urn down and spreads his arms wide.

"By faith Enoch was translated that he should not see death. He pleased Jahweh and walked with him and was not found because Jahweh lifted him to heaven."

A chorus of amens rises from the nodding listeners.

Enoch pounds his fist on the pulpit.

"Jahweh took him to protect him! Soon after, a flood destroyed the world and only eight souls were saved."

Enoch takes an exaggerated deep breath.

"Eight souls!"

The room turns deathly silent.

"Jahweh's word says that the mouths of two witnesses shall establish truth. In the last days he will give power to his two witnesses to prophesy one thousand two hundred and sixty days clothed in sackcloth. The mystery of the two witnesses is now revealed. The first Enoch prophesied and condemned the world and was taken before the flood, so now I-the second Enoch-will do the same and Jahweh will take me and condemn the world once more!"

Brother Enoch releases another deep breath.

"The prophet Jonah was three days in the belly of the great fish and the son of man was three days and nights in the tomb. Both came forth as redeemers, Jonah to the Ninevites and Jesus to the world. But this wicked generation cannot be redeemed! Jahweh has told me-Brother Enoch, to prepare the way of the Lord. As he destroyed the earth with a great flood, he will destroy the false prophets and deceivers-this time with fire! The members of Satan's synagogue have hardened their hearts and will not repent! And they shall be thrust into the lake of fire with the fearful, the unbelievers, the abominable, murderers, whoremongers, sorcerers, idolaters, and all liars!"

Enoch unscrews the urn; he raises it over his head with both hands.

"This is the cup of Jahweh's wrath!" he shouts, "Take from it and prepare the way of the Lord. And now I the second Enoch do repent in sackcloth and ashes hereby condemning the world."

Eyes tightly closed he tilts the urn-spilling a cloud of powdery ashes on his head and tunic.

Covered in ash, he leaves the pulpit and shuffles down the aisle scattering handfuls of leftover ash on the congregation, including the visitor.

"And now Jahweh's servants these commandments are for you. Go up against the inhabitants of Satan's seat and against the false teachers and deceivers, waste and utterly destroy them. And ye shall tread down the wicked and they shall be ashes under the soles of your feet!"

Enoch pours the remaining ashes on the floor, grinding the pile with his shoe.

Using the screaming and dancing members as a screen, the visitor slips out the door unnoticed.

Walking stiffly the visitor brushes stubborn ashes from his sport coat sleeves.

A familiar car waits for him at a nearby bus stop.

He opens the door and flops in the passenger seat.

"Was Keitel there?"

Manfred Schollner nods.

"He was seated next to Frau Obermayer."

"He lied to me." Lars shakes his head.

"Did you spot Nowak?"

"He was there too, and you were right," Schollner mutters, "Brother Enoch is a kook."

---

## Friday: Morning

Picking through boxes of fresh fruits and vegetables stacked outside *Amir's Fruchtmarkt*, Lars pays for a clear plastic bag filled with yellowing bananas.

He peels one and wanders down Munchener Strasse, stopping at *Neustart Employment Services*.

---

"Petr Nowak started last month as a Strassenbahn driver trainee." The front desk receptionist says.

"Is he still working?"

"No sir he quit two days ago."

Lars frowns. "Did he have references?"

She taps her computer keyboard in a flurry of fingers.

"He did list an address."

---

## Friday: Late Afternoon

GESCHLOSSEN AUS DEM GESCHÄFT!
"Closed? Out of business?"

Glaring at the sign in the Deutschland Novelties and Souvenir Exports window, Lars slams the security padlock against the door and stalks back to the Saab.

Frau Attiger's text chimes as he pulls up to his apartment.

*Nigel Trotter didn't show for work this morning.*

· ✦✦✦✦ ·

## Saturday: Seven A.M.

Holding the Frankfurter Allegemeine at eye level Lars watches *46 Westendstrasse* through the Saab's fogging windshield.

His intermittent wipers slosh away a steady drizzle.

He quickly turns them off-approaching milky headlights pierce the mist rising from the street.

He slides down in his seat watching a slow-moving white van roll past and parallel park between two cars.

The idling van's passenger door opens.

Peeking over his steering wheel Lars snaps Petr Nowak's picture before he pulls a hoodie over his head and dashes to the apartment.

Ten minutes later he snaps another picture of Nowak with a backpack slung over his shoulder.

Nowak holds the van door open-his face turning.

*Scheisse! Looking directly at me!*

Heart racing, Lars inches further down behind his steering wheel.

He blows out a sigh when the van slowly drives away.

· ✦✦✦✦ ·

## SATURDAY AFTERNOON

"I told you we suck; three nothing." Lars mutters.

Stuck in traffic leaving Frankfurt's Commerzbank-Arena, he glances at Oom filing her nails.

"You're quiet, what's the matter?"

She sighs and stares out the passenger window.

"Sorry just thinking about Frau M."

Her jaw trembles, she shields her face shuddering and convulsing in tears.

Lars gently grips her hand.

"I understand Oom, I have to suppress violent murders as much as the losses closest to me, but they end up merging together in a blur. I've been struggling with that lately and that's why I need you to balance me."

He keeps driving, blinking away his own tears.

# CHAPTER FORTY-SIX

"**A** LOT MORE STATIC TONIGHT."

A beer in one hand Lars fine tunes his shortwave.

Brother Enoch's voice finally filters through.

"...*Jesus warned his disciples to beware of the leaven of the Pharisees and Sadducees. They deceived the people then just as now. These last days' scoffers walk after their own lusts. They are like their master Satan seeking to devour. They have changed truth for lies, and worship and serve the creature more than the Creator!*"

"*Beware of dogs, beware of sinners that walk among us, busybodies whose mouths must be stopped! Their throats are open tombs, their tongues utter deceit. The poison of asps is under their lips. Calling themselves wise, these false teachers subvert houses and overthrow the faith of some!*"

"*But we shall not fear for Jahweh will punish them that trouble us. I turn to the words of the first Enoch.*"

Brother Enoch's voice lowers. Lars imagines him reading from a book.

"*Then shall children be slain with their mothers and sons with their fathers. And the punishment of the Lord of spirits shall continue upon them, the punishment of the Lord of spirits shall not be in vain...*"

A burst of static cuts him off, other garbled voices fade in and out, Enoch finally breaks through clearly.

*"...This is the vision Enoch saw before being taken and now I the second Enoch the second golden candlestick have seen the same vision. The Old Testament Jahweh was a god of war smiting his enemies wherever he went. He drowned Pharaoh's armies in the Red Sea. He destroyed mighty Jericho. He slaughtered the Baal worshippers in their own temple. He led Israel forth conquering the Hittites, the Amorites, the Jebusites, and the Canaanites-"*

More fuzzy static, more choppy voices.

Lars adjusts the antenna trying different positions.

*"...So now when we find ourselves surrounded...by our adversaries, we must do as Jesus said. When they persecute you in one city...flee to another. When the second Enoch...is taken up then...shall the judgment begin.... He will go forth leading us-the modern Israelites to victory over our enemies and a remnant shall follow him to a land flowing with milk and honey!"*

"Do you know what time it is?" Hauptmann Muller says in a scratchy voice.

"Sorry to wake you sir, but this couldn't wait. I listened to Brother Enoch's latest message. I'm no bible expert but I think he was calling for another killing or hinting of leaving."

"Right away?"

"I'm not sure."

"Call me back when you are."

His mouth open, Lars stares at the silent phone in his palm.

---

## SUNDAY MORNING: BOCKENHEIM

"Lars, it's so nice to see you again."

"Ahh, Frau Geiger, good to see you as well."

Lars bows respectfully, offering his hand.

She grips a rail and gingerly descends the Saint Elizabeth church's concrete steps.

"I must have missed you inside."

"I didn't attend Mass. I had confession with the assistant priest."

Frau Geiger nods with an approving smile.

"So how are you?"

"I am coming to terms with my brother's departure."

"You took the important first step. Continue to pray for his soul. I will beseech Mother Mary for you as well."

Her fingers caress the gold rosary around her neck.

"Thank you." Lars says head down in respect.

"Are you still working on the killings?"

"Yes, and I hope to have an arrest soon."

"You will, God will reward your determination."

"Excuse me."

He smiles and brings his ringing cell phone to his ear.

"Kubach here."

"Lars this is officer Detweiler. I'm headed to the Latter Rain Tabernacle; we got a protester out front."

"Did you say the Latter Rain Tabernacle?"

"That is affirmative."

"I'm on the way."

He slides the phone in his pocket and hugs her.

"Frau Geiger, I'm sorry, but I'm needed on an urgent call."

---

Lars slams his car door and races to Officer Detweiler's side.

"What's going on?" he says between breaths.

"I just got here myself. Someone in the church called about him."

Lars follows Detweiler's eyes to a young man pacing on the Latter Rain Tabernacle's sidewalk.

An object wrapped in brown paper juts out of his backpack.

Lars freezes, his mind racing with rapid images.

*The same backpack from yesterday! What's inside? a bomb? a gun? a skateboard?*

"He's Petr Nowak one of the sect members." he blurts out, amazed at his calm voice.

"Sir, you need to leave the area." Detweiler says.

Pastor Kruge cracks the door open and peeks out.

Stepping cautiously toward Nowak, Detweiler motions furiously at Kruge to go back inside.

Nowak's left cheek twitches–his trembling hand reaches in his sweatpants.

"He's armed." Lars says, his eyes riveted to a shiny metallic handle jutting from the waistband.

Close enough to make a tackle, Detweiler unsnaps his holster, pulling out his service pistol.

"Sir put your hands where I can see them."

In a heart stopping second, Nowak yanks out a revolver.

"The suicide weapon," Lars hisses, "He's here to start a massacre!"

Arms outstretched, both hands gripping his pistol, Detweiler aims at Nowak.

"Put the weapon down now!" He yells.

"Put it down!" Lars joins in.

Nowak slowly raises his hands.

*Good he's giving up.*

From the corner of his eye, Lars spots an approaching elderly couple. He is too late motioning them away.

The woman's scream merges with an ear-splitting pop.

The downy haired man pulls his wife's hand-shielding her he shuffles away as fast as his old legs will allow.

*Detweiler shot him!*

Lars spins around, his wide eyes locked on the slow-motion sequence.

A bloody spraying halo...the revolver clattering on the sidewalk... Nowak pitching face forward like a fresh cut tree.

His body hits the ground with a thud, a dark blood pool spreads on the sidewalk under his head.

"He shot himself." Detweiler says in a choked voice.

Lars immediately crouches over Nowak's body, feeling for a pulse. He looks up at Detweiler's ashen face and blood-spattered uniform and slowly shakes his head.

Distant wailing police sirens break the eerie calm.

—————— ‹‹‹‹‹‹‹ ——————

## SUNDAY AFTERNOON: BAHNHOFSVIERTEL POLIZEI STATION

"Come in."

His face grim, Hauptmann Muller pushes aside a stack of papers and motions Lars to the armchair.

"Detective Kubach this incident is all over Germany. Shurtzmann called, he spent most of the morning pleading with the media to keep it from going international."

Lars nods solemnly. "I understand sir."

Burying his forehead in both hands Muller stares down at his desk. "I don't want to hear I told you so, but who was it?"

"Petr Nowak, I made the official id at the hospital."

"Is there any chance he planned it alone?"

"I doubt it, beside the guns in his backpack I found this."

He hands Muller a crumpled scrap of paper.

"Smite the shepherd, and the sheep shall be scattered. What does that mean?"

"It's Zechariah thirteen seven. From my limited Bible knowledge, I would say it is a coded order to kill pastor Kruge."

"Are you sure?"

"I talked with him recently. Brother Enoch led a split from his church over doctrinal disputes. I think this was a revenge attempt."

"Why bring attention like this when you are already under suspicion?"

"Yesterday, I photographed Nowak leaving the cult address with the same backpack. Norman Ainsworth dropped him off and left with him.

Nowak seemed to abort the attempt when we showed up. I'm wondering if Ainsworth knew of the guns he had."

Muller massages his eyes and his nose; he stares at his desk and speaks slowly, almost whispering.

"I'm not supposed to tell you this. Shurtzmann had the feds take over to find out how the killers obtained the guns. And…they were very curious about your report's mention of an Interpol Blue notice. Right now, I'd rather not ask."

"I might have a way to reign in Jahweh's warriors."

"I'm listening."

"Brother Enoch's rants could be considered threats of violence."

"I agree but it's way too borderline to prove."

"There is another way-his shortwave broadcasts have a lot of bleed over. I spotted what looks like a homemade antenna behind his apartment. Illegal transmissions are reason enough for a search."

"I can't authorize anything without some type of proof."

"We could check to see if he's licensed." Lars says his voice prodding.

Muller leans back, folding his hands on his stomach, pursing his lips he gazes thoughtfully at the ceiling.

"I have a friend in Deutsche Telekom who can verify if the signal is legal. I'll contact him. In the meantime, we've got some explaining to do."

# CHAPTER FORTY-SEVEN

*THE KAISER BISTRO*: SUNDAY EVENING

TAGESSCHAU NEWS ANCHOR MATTHIAS STAHL straightens his tie, taps a stack of papers on his desk and looks directly into the camera.

His arms folded on the bar counter Lars watches the wall mounted flat screen, waiting for the inevitable *Media Exclusiv.*

Sure enough, it's the opening story, delivered as always in Stahl's monotone German.

"Guten Abend mein Damen und Herren. Matthias Stahl reporting. Frankfurt–the Polizei thwarted a potential mass shooting at the Latter Rain Tabernacle in Bornheim Sunday morning. The unidentified suspect shot himself after a tense standoff. Polizei Sergeant Jurgen Detweiler gave this account at the scene."

The screen switches to Detweiler's blanched face.

"We responded to a call about a man harassing church members. He refused multiple orders to leave the area."

His halting voice cracks with emotion.

"It happened so fast. He pulled out the weapon and used it before we could react."

The screen returns to Matthias Stahl.

"For more details we now take you to the Polizeipräsidium."

The screen switches to Polizeipräsident Shurtzmann's haggard face besieged by a sea of extended boom microphones and flashing cameras.

"The suspect's backpack contained a shotgun, a second pistol and close to a hundred rounds of ammunition."

"Was he planning a massacre?" several reporters' voices shout at once.

"We can't be certain yet; the investigation is ongoing. Thank you for your time."

The screen returns to Stahl's stern face.

"When asked if the incident might be related to a series of recent murders, detective Lars Kubach had no comment."

Lars checks an incoming text.

*Still no work I'm free tonight, come over.*

He empties his Hefe Weisen and signals the bartender.

## THREE A.M.

Hunched over the edge of the bed with a towel wrapped around his waist Lars answers his cell phone.

"Kubach here."

"Detective Kubach be in my office in a half hour."

"Yes sir."

Lars shrugs at Oom lying naked next to him.

"I hear him, go on I will wait for you."

Oom winks and wraps herself in her sheet.

## BAHNHOFSVIERTEL POLIZEI STATION

Hauptmann Muller tosses Lars a sealed envelope.

"Look inside."

"Is this what I think it is?"

Muller nods.

"A raid approved by Shurtzmann and the BKA earlier tonight."

"How did they approve it so fast?"

"When contacted about Norman Ainsworth, Scotland Yard requested his immediate arrest for identity fraud. The SEK will conduct the raid. They believe Ainsworth or Brother Enoch may be the gun suppliers. I want you to assist them."

"Ok sir."

"There's more. My Deutsch Telekom contact checked Brother Enoch's broadcast. He's not licensed, and his signal interferes with other frequencies."

"Shurtzmann said we are going all in on this raid. We're going after identity fraud, radio piracy, and conspiracy to supply weapons, whatever else we find will be a bonus. We move in at six am. I want you with them and I want Ainsworth and Enoch alive. At that point we'll prove or disprove their connection to the murders."

# CHAPTER FORTY-EIGHT

INSIDE A WINDOWLESS BLACK VAN, Lars and Hauptmann Stieg Huffner hover over a hand drawn floorplan.

"The apartment has three floors. Floor one was renovated into an open worship bay. Floor two should be individual living rooms and I'm guessing floor three is where brother Enoch does his broadcast."

Huffner briefly lifts his black Polizei mask.

"Are they armed?"

"It's possible."

Huffner frowns. A voice crackles in his headset.

"Both teams are in position sir."

"Let's go. I want Enoch and Norman Ainsworth untouched."

———————•◆◆◆◆•———————

Two battering ram hits splinter the front door, busting it off the hinges.

Black masked officers in body armor and helmets spread out inside pointing flashlights and assault rifles in all directions.

Several officers stop and back up, their gun's red lasers aimed at an open stairwell door.

Holding a pistol at his temple, Norman Ainsworth slowly descends the steps.

His wicked smile vanishes when Lars and Huffner enter.

"Lower your weapons men." Huffner orders with a raised arm.

Lars quickly scans the floor-no keyboard, folding chairs, or tables, just Ainsworth standing where the pulpit used to be.

"Where is Enoch?" Lars barks.

His pallid face brightly lit by multiple flashlights Ainsworth's ghoulish smile returns.

"And Enoch walked with God and was not for God took him. These are the two candlesticks standing before God."

"Norman Ainsworth you are under arrest for identity theft." Huffner says loudly.

Ainsworth's mocking laugh echoes in the tense quiet room.

"It's so easy. Take the dregs of society, the sick, the desperate. They have nothing to live for anyway and are less likely to care about life, perfect recruits."

"Arrest him." Huffner orders.

The officers surround Ainsworth in a semi-circle.

Ainsworth cocks the pistol.

"Put the gun down now!" multiple voices shout.

Lars raises his hands to calm them.

*Not another suicide!*

"And Enoch the seventh from Adam…"

Ainsworth squeezes the trigger.

"Nooo…" Lars yells.

Ainsworth's eyes widen like saucers, pulpy brain chunks spray behind him; he staggers backward, the Beretta slipping from his limp hand.

His body hits the floor with a sickening thump.

Lars jerks his face away.

"Fuck!" he yells with his head in his hands.

A police officer with a terror-stricken face, pushes past the stunned officers; his hands trembling he pulls Lars aside, whispering in his ear.

"Detective I think you should see this."

Twenty minutes later Hauptmann Muller slams his car door and hurriedly follows Huffner inside.

"Sir I think Detective Kubach is better suited to show you what we found. He's on the second floor."

Back turned, his head down, Lars stands on the top stair.

Muller takes one hesitant stair at a time.

"Hauptmann Huffner said you have something to show me?"

"I wish I didn't have to."

He turns, his haunted face confirming Muller's rising fear.

---

"Oh my God." Muller gasps.

He silently counts fifteen face-up bodies in one long row down the tiled hallway.

His head spinning Lars walks past each body arranged identically– eyes closed, legs together, arms folded across the chest.

He recognizes the stork...the elderly usher...

Tears welling in his eyes he stops at the bodies of Gunnar Weiss and Joshua Morgan.

"A ritual suicide." he says in a choked voice.

A hand covering his mouth, Muller manages a horrified nod.

# CHAPTER FORTY-NINE

A COPY OF THE *FRANKFURTER TAGBLATT* folded under his arm Lars pulls out a chair in *Sylvia's Kaffee Shoppe*.

--- ◆◆◆◆ ---

## DOOMSDAY CULT LEADER KILLED IN STANDOFF

Frankfurt, Germany – The leader of an extremist religious sect was killed in a standoff with the Polizei early this morning. The sixty-eight-year-old man is tentatively identified as Nigel Trotter. Little is known about his background, but Polizei reports indicate he was inciting the sect to "subversive behavior using a pirated radio broadcast."

In a brief statement Polizei Hauptmann Tobias Muller said the members vandalized local businesses including Club Bacchus where popular owner Teddy van Halst was slain. He stopped short of admitting the incidents were related.

"We have no reason to connect the sect's activity to Mister Van Halst's savage killing by a troubled young man."

When asked why reporters were restricted to the sidewalk Hauptmann Muller said the incident was a security matter and the building was still being searched.

Commenting on several ambulances and Polizei vans at the scene he cited "extra precautions had been taken," and would not elaborate further.

⁕⁕⁕⁕⁕

"Guten Morgen Lars. I brought breakfast."

Muller sets down two cups of steaming coffee with two cheese bagels and pulls out a chair.

His red eyes puffy from sleeplessness, Lars stirs in a mini cup of cream and takes a tentative sip.

"The headline wasn't too sensational." Muller says.

"Sooner or later sir, someone will discover the truth. At least five members including Brother Enoch, Thorsten Keitel, and doctor Kolb are still missing."

"It's the best I could do for now. We still have to explain the bodies. What else did you find?"

"Enoch broadcasted from an upstairs room converted into a studio. We found a transmitter kit, a microphone, a headset, and boxes of wires. The antenna was crudely mounted outside the building. But I have a question sir."

"Go ahead."

"Why did you give the media Nigel Trotter's name?"

"I want this Enoch character to believe we misidentified the body in our hurry to close the case. That way he will think he's safe to surface later. I've already pressed Shurtzmann to do the same-at least for now."

Muller taps his temple, Lars shudders at the gesture.

"So now what?"

"Shurtzmann is holding a press conference as we speak. There is certain to be a firestorm of speculation and conspiracy theories. He ordered me to give you an immediate leave of absence due to PTSD and burnout."

"Are you serious?"

"One month effective today with full pay and benefits. And no media contact whatsoever. And Lars…"

Muller sighs.

"I apologize for being so hard on you during this case. I know your reputation as a good detective, but I thought you were slipping and losing your focus. I learned not to underestimate your methods and hunches. Now that it's over I want you back as good as new."

"I will, but I have one unrelated matter."

"And that is?"

"Oom wants her business back."

## WEDNESDAY EDITION, FRANKFURTER ALLGEMEINE ZEITUNG

## SIXTEEN DEAD IN CULT SUICIDE

Frankfurt, Germany – Sixteen members of a fringe sect identified as Jahweh's Warriors were found dead after police raided their apartment Monday morning. Officers found the bodies after a shootout with the sect leader.

"It appears the members were deceased before the raid. Cause of death remains undetermined, and our investigation is ongoing." Polizeipräsident Rheinhart Shurtzmann said.

Herr Shurtzmann attributed the delay in reporting the bodies to confusion that other members may have still been hiding in the apartment which was locked down "until we determined there was no further danger." He added.

The mass suicide is one of Germany's worst ever and is compared to Switzerland's October 1994 Order of the Solar Temple mass suicides where twenty-three members were found dead in the village of Cheiry. Twenty-five bodies were found hours later in another village. In all seventy-four were found dead over a three-year period.

Jahweh's Warriors were under the radar until recently. Reports claim the members believed in a prophetic doomsday scenario mentioned in the Book of Revelation.

When asked if there were any survivors Herr Shurtzmann said. "We are certain the deceased were the group's core members. All sect materials and belongings will be checked down to the finest detail."

———— ⋅⁺⁺✦⁺⁺⋅ ————

## BOCKENHEIM: ONE WEEK LATER

## MUSEUMSUFERFEST A ROUSING SUCCESS

### Record Crowds Despite Recent City Troubles
Lars smiles at the Frankfurter Allgemeine headline.

Waiting for the free Wi-Fi to connect he sips coffee at the *König Café*, the only Bäckerei open before seven A.M.

His day is planned, a five-kilometer run and a grueling round of calisthenics at *Hoyer's* athletic club.

But first, his unopened emails.

*From: Gerhard Schmidt Coroner:*

*Cult members killed by a mass overdose of Halodan and sleeping pills. Two members, Bernd Mielke & Gunnar Weiss recently filled prescriptions.*

*From: GRosenblatt@euromail:*

*I have two tickets for the annual creatures of the night exhibition, would you like to go? Just my saying thanks for your good work. Giselle*

A Strassenbahn glides past the café window, he frowns at the *Frankfurter Tagblatt* slogan on the side.

*"WIR FINDEN DIE WAHRHEIT!" "WE FIND THE TRUTH!"*

His phone chirps—an incoming text.

*Found the sect van in the airport parking garage.*

———— ⋅⁺⁺✦⁺⁺⋅ ————

Serious faced; Hauptmann Muller waits by the van with his arms crossed.

"It's unlocked. I want you to look through it first."

"I thought I was supposed to be stressed out." Lars says.

Waiting in his cruiser, Detweiler hides his slick grin behind his notepad.

Scrunching his nose Lars fans away stale cigarette odor and clicks on his pencil flashlight.

The rear seats are gone; replaced by the pulpit, two stacks of folded metal chairs, and a pile of old protest signs.

*So, this is where they put everything.*

He picks up a pack of Haribo Gold Bears and a pamphlet on the passenger seat.

He flips through *Sin and the Human Condition*, and slides out a folded paper, handing it to Muller.

"A receipt for brick red spray paint from OBI?"

"This looks like a diversion." Lars says.

"What makes you say that?"

"It's too obvious. Whoever left it here unlocked with everything inside, wants us to think they took a flight in a hurry."

"We'll check the parking garage cameras and contact each carrier for any tickets purchased by the remaining sect members. I'll have forensics go through the van."

"Good idea sir and I would love to help but I am not feeling well, you know, stress and all."

Popping a red gummy bear in his mouth, Lars winks at Detweiler.

---

## LATER THE SAME DAY

"The Polizei are allowing me to reopen but without my workers." Oom says from her bathroom.

"What are you planning to do?"

"I have money saved. I'm going to Bangkok. I have friends there."

"You're coming back, right?"

"Of course, honey. When I return, I have bigger plans. first thing I do is change Eros Sauna name."

"That's good." Lars says, focused on sending a text.

*Giselle, thank you for your offer I would love to go. Perhaps we could have dinner afterwards? I know a good seafood place a few blocks from the zoo.*

He slips the phone in his pocket just as Oom opens the bathroom door.

# CHAPTER FIFTY

**ONE WEEK LATER: MAYOR ELKE HAGEN'S OFFICE**

**M**AYOR HAGEN'S PANELED OFFICE IS surprisingly modest. Behind her desk are two large potted leafy indoor plants, and a full bookshelf.

Spread out in front of her are two CONFIDENTIAL folders and a multipage report from the case.

Sharing her somber expression Lars sits on a shiny beige leather couch sandwiched between Polizeipräsident Shurtzmann and Hauptmann Muller.

on a shiny beige leather couch.

"Detective Kubach, I appreciate you coming in from your vacation, but I must admit that I find your report disturbing. Please tell me how you arrived at these conclusions."

Lars clears his throat.

"The coroner identified Herman Renke, Gunnar Weiss, and Joshua Morgan's parents. When I first interviewed them by phone, I was curious why they were vague about their children. I didn't realize that they were cult members."

Mayor Hagen flips to a page in the report.

"It says here they believed their children were living sacrifices?"

Biting his lip Lars glances sideways at Shurtzmann and Muller slowly shaking their heads.

"I found a large print Bible at the scene. I went over the highlighted verses with Pastor Kruge, he concluded that they emphasized the parent's determination not to make the same mistake Abraham made with his son Isaac."

"What mistake would that be?"

"In Genesis God ordered Abraham to sacrifice his son, but then changed his mind. Pastor Kruge connected the verses to show that the parents considered their children modern day versions of Isaac. Brother Enoch ordered them sacrificed for the world's sins like Jesus was."

"A really twisted way of thinking." Shurtzmann mutters.

Mayor Hagen agrees with a tight-lipped frown.

"There's more, other marked verses indicate Brother Enoch would disappear just like the Enoch in the Bible, once this happened his followers were to join him by committing suicide to be reunited with him and return to judge the earth."

Mayor Hagen folds her arms on her desk.

"Your report states that Norman Ainsworth and Doctor Kolb were recruited into the cult?"

"That is correct. Brother Enoch was a traveling preacher and they met at some point in Mannheim."

"And that's where they started together?"

"Yes, Brother Enoch brainwashed the parents to have them treated by Ainsworth and Kolb. A crude paper trail was created to blame mental illness and deflect suspicion away from the cult."

"Your report contains religious tracts kept as evidence. What did you do about them?"

"I contacted several places that sold them but unfortunately no one recalled any mass purchases."

"Now as for your case being taken over by the BKA. They raided *Deutschland Novelties and Souvenir Exports*. Thorsten Keitel was laundering money and possibly trafficking weapons too. They have alerted everyone-Interpol, Europol, Scotland Yard. Multiple warrants have been issued for his arrest. The BKA also discovered only a few of the members had cell phones. Do you have a theory about that?"

"Brother Enoch likely banned them, either to avoid them being tracked or as a form of control."

Hauptmann Muller clears his throat.

"Excuse me Ma'am there's something late to include in the report. Forensics found these in the sect van."

He holds up a sealed bag full of empty pill bottles.

"Doctor Kolb filled them two days before the suicides. Two Apotheke clerks said they remembered him."

Shurtzmann and Mayor Hagen take turns examining them.

"Halodan? Oh my god," Mayor Hagen gasps. "You were right detective Kubach."

Muller shakes his head without looking at Lars.

"We also reviewed the airport garage surveillance cameras. An unidentified male parked the van, left the garage and basically disappeared."

Mayor Hagen opens a folder on her desk

"The BKA's report states Norman Ainsworth was a master document forger, he purchased Nigel Trotter's information on the dark web and used his ID and credentials to work as a counselor for three hospitals. He was such a charmer that they unfortunately didn't do thorough background checks on him. Scotland Yard states the names Stoebel and Langenbrunner were fictitious. He also falsified Doctor Kolb's school transcripts and some of the cult member's passports."

"I came to the same conclusion. And since none of the surviving members boarded any flights it's likely they are using new identities elsewhere." Lars says.

Mayor Hagen takes a long drink of bottled water.

"That's what scares me."

## SIX MONTHS LATER: HAMBURG MENTAL HYGIENE CENTER

Doctor Helmut Larssen holds up a graduated syringe. A thin stream of clear liquid squirts from the needle tip.

"Are you sure the treatment will help him?" a voice says on his mobile phone.

"I understand your concern Frau Ratzner. Your son's concussion is bad. I have treated cases like this before. This is the best method for him. He should rest now."

"Thank you, doctor, I will visit him in the morning."

"No problem, Frau Ratzner, good night, and once again I apologize for waking you so early."

He ends the call and pats Joel's shoulder.

"Young man the injection will work right away. It should make you sleepy."

Doctor Larssen turns off the light and shuts the door.

Joel turns on his bedside radio. Feeling lightheaded he closes his eyes, listening to a baritone voice.

*"The Lord has declared you a priest forever after the order of Melchizedek and with Jehovah at your right hand he shall destroy the kings in the day of his wrath."*

Joel drifts to sleep with a wide smile. He likes *The Grand Mystic Order of Ephesus* and Prophet Melchizedek's courage to take a stand for Jehovah in this 'sin-stained world.' THE END

# German / English Equivalents

Non-Fiction Actual places phrases locations etc.

| German | English |
|---|---|
| Apfelwein | Apple wine |
| Apotheke | Drug store |
| Bahnhofsviertel | Train station district |
| Bockenheim / Bornheim | Frankfurt districts |
| Brotchen | bread roll |
| Bundesliga | Germany's pro soccer league |
| Bundeswehr | German Army |
| Die Toten Hosen | A famous German punk band |
| Dortmunder Union | A German beer brand |
| Eintracht Frankfurt | Frankfurt's pro soccer team |
| Guten Morgen/Tag/Abend | Good morning/day/evening |
| Hauptmann | Captain |
| Hauptbahnhof | Main train station |
| Haus Rosenblumen | House of roses/flowers |
| Hefeweizen | A German wheat beer |
| Herr | mister or sir |
| Imbiss | Food stand or small snack shop |
| Jaegerschnitzel | A type of breaded veal cutlet |
| Krankenhaus | Hospital |
| Maisel's Weisse | A German wheat beer brand |

| | |
|---|---|
| Museumsuferfest | Annual Frankfurt festival |
| Mein Damen und Herren | ladies and gentlemen |
| Palmengarten | Frankfurt's Botanical Garden |
| Polizeipräsidium | Police Headquarters |
| Polizeipräsident | Police President |
| Rotlichtviertel | Red light district |
| Strassenbahn | streetcar / trolley |
| Strasse | Street, name precedes the street. |
| Sachsenhausen | Frankfurt district |
| Sparkasse | Small bank like a credit union |
| Tagesschau *Morgenmagazine* | daily morning news show |
| U Bahn | Underground subway |
| Ubergangszentrum | Transition center/ shelter |

Printed in the United States
by Baker & Taylor Publisher Services

Printed in the United States
by Baker & Taylor Publisher Services